**Dreams
of the
Abandoned
Seducer**

Latin American
Women Writers

Series Editors

Jean Franco
Columbia University
Francine Masiello
University of California at Berkeley
Tununa Mercado
Mary Louise Pratt
Stanford University

Dreams of the Abandoned Seducer

(Sueños del
seductor
abandonado:
Novela vodevil)
Translated by
Cola Franzen
in collaboration
with the author

Alicia Borinsky

University of Nebraska Press, Lincoln and London

Originally published as *Sueños del seductor abandonado: Novela vodevil*, © 1995 by Alicia Borinsky
Translation and translator's note copyright © 1998 by the University of Nebraska Press. All rights reserved. Manufactured in the United States of America. ∞ The paper in this book meets the minimum requirements of American National Standard for Information Sciences—Permanence of Paper for Printed Library Materials, ANSI Z39.48-1984. Library of Congress Cataloging-in-Publication Data Borinsky, Alicia. [Sueños del seductor abandonado. English] Dreams of the abandoned seducer : vaudeville novel = Sueños del seductor abandonado : novela vodevil / Alicia Borinsky : translated by Cola Franzen in collaboration with the author. p. cm. — (Latin American women writers) ISBN 0-8032-1286-0 (cloth : alk. paper).—ISBN 0-8032-6144-6 (pbk. : alk. paper) I. Franzen, Cola. II. Title. III. Series.
PQ7798.12.0687S8413   1998
863-dc21   97-35668 CIP

Contents

Translator's Note vii

Dreams of the Abandoned Seducer 1

Interview with Alicia Borinsky 207

Translator's Note

Alicia Borinsky, born in Argentina and living in the United States, is a novelist, poet, and literary critic. She belongs to the generation of writers who came into their own after Borges and Puig. Borinsky's novelistic voice in its unrelenting humor proposes dizzying possibilities from a woman's perspective on society and the intricacies of love.

Dreams of the Abandoned Seducer holds out a rich sheaf of special pleasures, paradoxes, and puzzles for translator and reader. There are monologues, dialogues between characters and between author and reader, overheard telephone calls, talks and announcements on radio and TV, newspaper items directed to readers, bits of gossip, snatches of song lyrics, and sayings. The novel chronicles events unfolding in an invented city during a time that is today, or maybe tomorrow, where characters are running hard to achieve their various dreams, fancies, and wishes of every description. They hatch incongruous and ingenious plots that play out to hilarious, inexorable, ludicrous, or surprising ends.

Borinsky focuses on the ferment occurring in large present-day cities, the life being forged at this moment when so many are moving away from their homelands, and the free-market and new family configurations are reshaping so much of what used to be taken for granted. In the novel we find a world in flux, where everyone is looking for a shortcut, hoping at the very least to make it with the lottery. Both the city and the events recounted are invented but are clearly rooted in reality: it is their combination that provokes hilarity as well as surprising and unsettling effects. Humor is Borinsky's way of being serious; the serious undertones bubble up through cracks, creating laughter but also a kind of double take.

I had the good fortune to have the author's assiduous and expert help in this translation. Her contributions were invaluable. Together we have tried to recreate the dynamic atmosphere, pace, and tone of the novel and to reproduce the feeling of slang words and expressions, song snippets, and other elements that could not be "translated" strictly speaking but only rendered in a free version. We hope we have succeeded.

One of the things I love best about this book is that when the curtain comes down the story does not end. The door is left wide open. We're invited in to see where it leads. Who could resist?

Cola Franzen

**Dreams
of the
Abandoned
Seducer**

1
The characters I've identified from a distance just for you

Women and children first (pure fabrication, myself I'd be suspicious)

First of all she commits suicide because several problems are solved then and there:
  she won't have to ask anybody for anything
  stockings with runs will be over and done with
  nobody will ask for her date of birth
—Yes, but doesn't it seem premature to you that with no problem, no major concern, she should take off just like that, almost without ever having arrived?
—No. Because Mercedes always wanted to be a truly famous corpse. Ever since she started going to vaudeville shows she knew she'd make a splash someday one way or another, and that's how she hit upon the idea of throwing herself off the balcony wearing her tutu and her little tiara with all the rhinestones. She desperately wanted Shorty to miss her and succeeded so well the busybodies in the neighborhood began to make up romantic tales about them.
—Whatever, she killed herself too early.
—Don't believe it. Other women around here managed to disappear before. I can think of one, for example, who barely made it to the market and zap she was already in the other world.
  Dearest childhood friends:

                          that's how we talked in our club about certain women, those who would appear suddenly and then disappear without a trace, women escorted for a brief time or alone who would come one day wearing clothes bought in stores we'd never heard of and with purses holding things we could barely imagine. Women. Tough women and frail women hastily made up, all over thirty years old, whose vaginas enclosed the mystery of our differences. Where are they now? Where did they go? What did they do in the afternoons in the rooming houses, the hotel rooms, the apartments abandoned so furtively?
—I tell you that now she slips out with the old man across the way.
—I saw her in church making a play for the priest.

—She's a lesbian, she winked at me one day as she went by.
—The other day she was looking at herself in the mirror and crying; I think she turns into a striptease dancer at night but daylight makes her sad . . . her face looks almost as bored as our own.
—Her name is Mercedes
              Rosita
              Ana María
              Never do they call her Dumpling
or sweet love or chickie or baby or precious heart because she blends with all the other women, turns herself inside out, a glove with a thousand fingers, her tentacles suck us as she flees without leaving a forwarding address

THEY PARADE PARADE PAST IN A RUSH WATER FLUSHING TOWARD THE SEWER THEIR ODORS MAKE US DIZZY HERE IN THE CLUB WE SUMMON THEM SEEK THEM SO AS TO UNDERSTAND THEM

    Watch out, you picky foreign women, or we'll put you in a window display
    This is the chorus line and suicide is no solution
    The captain of the club holds all the keys. We thought about putting them all into sugar cones and eating them, licking them while we absorbed all their secrets and inhaled the fabulous aroma of all the bedding-downs, the darkness drop by drop, not leaving behind a single solitary hair to waft away.

now don't you go the way of Mercedes

She arrived a total mess. Mariano had given her the wrong telephone number, and when she called him from the station a guy who sounded drunk answered and told her to go to hell. To hell, as if she didn't have a round-trip ticket already. I'm back, love, I'm back from all that, stop all this nonsense and stop spouting naive metaphors.

They had a very lively conversation; the guy turned out to be a butcher with the hands of a surgeon who made her feel like a sacred cow, moo at his touch, praise him for everything without even knowing his name in that agitated and exhausting meeting that followed the telephone call. Mariano, beside himself, had asked if they had spotted her in the station and they said yes: "Yes, a rather slender woman, elegant, wearing dark-colored clothes, yes, around thirty-five years old, yes, yes a man came to meet her, no, I can't describe him, a guy like any other, oh yes, now I remember he came in a truck," so then he could begin to trace out the avenues of their misfortune.

—Mercedes, you know I've always loved and worshipped you. In my desk I keep little packages bulging with reminders of you
    sand from the park where we played as kids
    your first sanitary napkin
    the photograph of our engagement party
    the socks you gave me for my birthday
MERCEDES MERCEDES MERCEDES I've waited for you to the point of exhaustion every time you agreed to meet me in one of those stupid cafés where they give you anemic coffee with a lemon twist. I've seen you home after so many dances. Consoled you. Praised your worst habits. How can I forgive you, my dearest Mercedes. How can I tell you your betrayal doesn't matter to me even if it does away with all my hopes. You've left me because I didn't know how to tell you to go to hell and you went with the first man who could do it. Mercedes, you should be punished and now you tell me you're in love because of a chance telephone call. Don't

ask me to forgive you or assure me you'll fix your hair to go to my mother's house this evening, because I won't take you to celebrate my cousins' anniversary

MERCEDES MERCEDES MERCEDES

my beautiful sweetheart, middle-aged femme fatale of my bad luck, I won't let you gloat over your little adventure   your pleasures exasperate me   putting spray on your hair will do no good nor will asking for my forgiveness

—And who told you I wanted you to forgive me? Our engagement reaches the final form of its perfection, the brief pause for checking to make sure all the springs are in working order before looking back and turning into a pillar of salt.

I assure you that's exactly how Mercedes answered him. Never ever in her life had she been aware of the existence of sin. She walked past us looking straight ahead, with her slim skirt and high heels, lips red and hair loose. Mercedes with her fiancé was heading for the Botanical Garden. We'd follow a few steps behind until they sat down on a bench and started touching and kissing the minute it got the least bit dark. The newspaper he always carried in his pocket would get crumpled and he'd end up throwing it on the ground the better to keep it up. Truth is they were a bit chubby for that sort of scene. Thinking they were alone, they'd start panting; from the shrubbery we could see little drops of sweat on Mariano's forehead and mascara smudging Mercedes's cheeks.

Mercedes doesn't bother to look at us as she walks by because she doesn't care about little girls. She's not at all like those other women forever posing as gushing mamas.

We expect nothing from her. She didn't want to strike up a friendship or know what sort of work our papa did, what our mama's maiden name was. None of that mattered to Mercedes because we know that no children will be born of her body; her figure and her clothes have been fixed for all time.

IF THEY WOULD ONLY MOVE TO ANOTHER NEIGHBOR-

HOOD IF ONLY THEY WOULD TEAR DOWN THAT ROOM-
ING HOUSE IF AT LEAST THEY WOULD RENT IT ONLY
TO SINGLE MEN I'VE HAD IT UP TO HERE WITH THOSE
LOOSE WOMEN. Mamas talking on the telephone. Mamas in the hallways. Mamas sheltering us from the terrible silence surrounding Mercedes and her fall.

—Mariano, Mariano, don't quiz me and don't beg to see me. Your salary raise means little or nothing to me, Mariano. And I'm not really impressed by your faithfulness. If you love me, fine, be my guest. If you hate me, ditto. My dear Mariano: after the theater, the movie, and the pizza I'll give your confessions back to you done up in a little Christmas package.

It was the doorman who saw her jump and assured me she was a very neat young lady and that no, he couldn't let us see her clothes or enter her room because of strict orders from the police. Mariano, somewhat pale, arrived at the rooming house with an elderly woman and we didn't have a clue as to what they did inside although we didn't take our eyes off the place. When he left two hours later carrying a package wrapped in brown paper under his arm, Mariano looked like any father, his air of happy-go-lucky lover gone and with a noticeable paunch when you looked at him sideways. The elderly woman must have stayed behind to clean the room, that's what my mama said.

sick, crazy women, how can they keep it up

She studied the faces of the other women in the rooming house and then applied her make-up, careful to avoid the smallest mistake. Her all but endless wary suspicions had turned her into a meek little flower that shied away from getting caught up in anything new. She always wore heels. The day we saw her for the first time with her small worn brown suitcase we all decided she was probably poor, that her life had come to such a pass because of the death of parents and friends; we pitied her for her bad luck and called her Rosita because it went so well with her flowered blouse and the shade of her lipstick.

The doctor on the corner had a large mysterious clientele. Each patient would give a short ring of the doorbell then disappear inside. Every two hours, three afternoons a week, men and women dressed with varying degrees of formality came to be seen by him from miles away (we knew because of how they hesitated about which bus to take after their appointments or the way they often parked in reserved spaces or suddenly turned the wrong way against the traffic). NERVOUS AND MENTAL DISORDERS. Dr. Bermúdez, temples almost white, smiled absent-mindedly at the children who passed by his house on Saturday afternoons when he would appear with his son Miguel, a skinny toothy preadolescent, face pale like all kids who go to private schools.

Rosita began to go to Dr. Bermúdez's office very soon. It's hard to tell if she moved to our neighborhood because of him or if she just happened to notice the plaque on the door after one of her daily walks and decided to ask for an appointment.

How you would run about, Rosita, shouting obscenities in the square
How you ripped your clothes that Sunday after mass
How we stared at you not understanding what you were saying
Where were you going made up with such perfection?
Was someone waiting for you in a street you were still searching for?

HOWL HOWLS OF ROSITA WHO DOESN'T SPEAK TO US AND CAN'T STAND US

—Bermúdez drove her crazy. He's a pervert.
—It's enough to look at Miguel's face, poor thing; if only the mother were still alive.
—Berta must be turning over in her grave; may she rest in peace.
—A kid who should've had his teeth straightened.
—A kid who could've gone to the school here in the neighborhood instead of who knows what boarding school with priests.
—A kid who could've had rosy cheeks, been a worthy son of our dear friend; we could've helped raise him and one day he could've married one of our daughters.
—A kid with a future and now the father doesn't even speak to us. They're all the same. They get crazier than their patients. Or maybe they were that way to start with. Doctor—my eye. Worse than any quack. What kind of medicine is it that makes patients talk and never ever looks at their body. They say it's nothing but pure chitchat. You talk about anything at all and that's it. A real doctor is somebody who heals you with medicine and examinations, who checks you, one that if you go in sick one day you'll come out well, cheered up with your prescription for the pharmacy and the advice to get some exercise although some say total rest is better; why can't they make up their minds about it. And now imagine that poor woman who lives in the rooming house. What did he do to her: one minute she's running around crazier than a loon and the next she's walking along very properly and not talking to herself.
—The man in the bakery says she's a very nice person who hardly says a word when someone jumps the line ahead of her.
—Always so neat.
—Do you think she could be dangerous?

—I would call the police when she has those attacks, but then they'd put her away and that would make me feel so bad.
—Such an elegant woman.

When we came back from summer vacation, Rosita was no longer in the rooming house. It seems she'd had a difficult summer. Dr. Bermúdez was called urgently by the neighbors to calm her down one hot and rainy afternoon when she tried to scratch a cat that had taken shelter in the doorway of the rooming house, and the cat made such a racket it disturbed the siesta. Rosita yowled and yowled until the sedative took effect, and it took three of them to carry her to Dr. Bermúdez's office.

> **Let her come out**
> > **let her tell us what has happened to her**
>
> **let us see her**
>
> **let the patients who are suffering tell us what we are missing and what we have too much of**
>
> **please**
>
> > **let us see her**
> > > **let's guess what happens behind the door**

Rosita now walked like a robot when she once again crossed the street to the rooming house. Legs half-rigid, she went goose-stepping along to buy cookies at the store. No make-up. She'd been reduced to the bare truth of her movements. Every afternoon at five she would walk along the same streets and take a bus, her face a blank. At night we would see her return, a grimace resembling a smile on her face, key in hand ready to open the door.

Rosita is the private tutor in the kindergarten of a fabulously rich man who doesn't want his son mixing with the poor misfits who swarm in the streets.

Rosita is a bolero singer who crossdresses as a robot as soon as she finishes the lyrics.

Rosita has children scattered around various parts of the city and visits them on the sly so their fathers won't know she didn't actually die giving birth.

Rosita pretends to be a woman but when she goes into her room she growls and howls, mane loosened, right next door to us with all our misfortunes, daring lioness, panther, hieratic figure.

Star of our world, the spotlight blinds us and veils her. She doesn't care for us but how we yearn for her. She does not kiss us but how many questions we could've asked her.

   ATTENTION FABULOUS FRIENDS OF MY EMBRACES SHE GOOSE-STEPS DOWN THE SIDE STREETS OF ALL THE NEIGHBORHOODS WEARS A WATCH THAT KEEPS OUR TIME
      WE ALL HAVE A DATE WITH ROSITA
      WE WILL ARRIVE BEFORE THE CURTAIN GOES UP

Where Dr. Bermúdez's house used to stand they put up a beauty shop, after he and his son were convinced by a crass realtor that it was better to go live in a higher-class neighborhood where there'd be even more sick people able to pay the sky-high fees he demanded now that the news of his successful treatment of Rosita had got around and was bringing in patients by the carload.

somewhere somebody is always making love

—Now I've showed you my teeth. Mouth open, head back, neck stiff. I've given you all my cancelled dentist's appointments, all the candies still drilling holes in me. My bacteria are yours. In plain view. I hide nothing from you and give you all. What more can you ask for? A woman is not measured by inches of skin offered at twilight. A woman is not taken just like that in beds smeared by sweat, semen, hairs plucked out absent-mindedly. No. No. And no. That's why I tell you to do whatever you please. Look at me as I've never seen myself before. Treasure, succulent treasure that I didn't taste, bite deliberately set on the table, howling bolero of my offering.

—Twice crazed but alone like nobody else. I invite you to travel with me to foreign places where they speak languages that have no dictionaries, countries forever exotic where even exiles dare not go because there are no journalists, no souvenir shops, no telephones for making long-distance calls. They'll think we're perfect lovers.

   I will examine you

   we'll stretch to our limits

   we'll put cute little bows on you

   at night the ardor of my embrace will be an anonymous banner you can carry to any dream whatsoever   it will last you hours after I rush out of bed to read the newspaper and go to work at the office

   at night it will be your lot to be always another teenage sweetheart of my first dances   hot little girl   acne-faced   mouth always longing   always another   I will erase your other lives and that's why we wont be able to tell when you leave

They talk and think that way because they haven't yet taken in the complexity of business deals that their ardor will make possible. They're romantic and sentimental. They're startled if we turn on the light because they love each other with exclusive innocence, but they'll change. We know they will. And it will happen so soon it will take them a lifetime to remember this moment.

Here comes our star!

She's outside. Sitting before the window as though expecting news from the house. She wants the house to send her a letter. It's too dark there, dust has been gathering for months. Nothing or nobody to give her a sign. But she persists. Eyes fixed. Knitting in hand. In anguish at times. Elated when you come near and kiss her on the forehead. Electricity runs through her and invites you. To make love with the sweet old lady. Enter into her looniness. Be the telegram she's waiting for. Once and for all do away with her muteness and your own.

He couldn't do it. He gathered up her things, called the police, and asked them to take her to the Institute. She put up no resistance. On the contrary. She threw him a provocative glance, lifted her dress revealing the thick forest where he recognized little red riding hood walking innocently toward that perfect tryst, deluded by the wolf's already moist teeth   the fruit in the basket sweet and rotten thrown over a cliff   little red riding hood in the wildest moment of her walk saying yes   stunned by the gleam of danger and the unusually sharp profile of the grandmother's face the bites and the hunter's misunderstanding   home sweet home   the disappointing jam after the feast

That's what he saw in the old woman's forest as she winked at him and danced a cancan while they carried her away. She already knew then she'd find perfect accomplices, resolute spies made to order for her wishes. So she slowly completed the Institute's questionnaire with the typical tediousness of the generation that makes us into detectives, public accountants, medical specialists.

Don't touch me and don't poke your fingers in my ears or up my ass. I see them everywhere I look. Sons of bitches. Out to take advantage. Psychiatrists. Speculators. Crooks. Don't touch me, the old lady was saying flirtatiously. And he already in the center of her lie barely resisted her malicious cunning charm.

They took her away and he felt no pity for her

—Papers, please. No, I don't mean fudge or caramel wrappers. Please, madam, remember, the infirmary has been closed for months and now hordes of women worse off than you are milling around the door. Papers. We want to know who you are. We have to enter your name in the register. Make a file. Give it a number and a name so you'll be eligible to receive cookies. So we can steal toilet paper. So when we go home every pocket will proclaim our victory: they think they pay us very little, think they're exploiting us, but we're hustlers, independent, we take a gamble on life like anyone else. Let's go, hurry, it's getting late. Madam, madam, your papers. We're not interested in the gossip about the grocer.

—Nuttier than the woman yesterday, but appealing. She doesn't understand but looks straight at you. And if it wasn't for those yellow teeth, I'd say she ate rich gooey things as a kid. Look at those cheeks, they must have been really stuffed with the very expensive goodies like they sell in those fancy pastry shops downtown. Bitch, and now we're the ones who have to take care of her. Burden. Burden. What a burden. Who gives you the right to burst out laughing? Sarcastic old fool, pretending to be crazy just to be more of a pain in the ass. Your little world must be pure fantasy. Come on, stop that singing.

—Look, I found the paper. Josefina, her name is Josefina de la Puente.

—Señora de la Puente, please be so kind as to sign this sheet and with this number, you'll go straight to the shower for me; we'll give you a clean uniform, and if you wish, go on with your litany that nobody's ever got out of this place.

—What's that she's singing? All day long, the same thing. But she'll get tired. Our famous diet will do away with the jokes and the tunes.

—Go and take the music with you to the shower, dear Señora de la Puente. And don't beam with such happiness, because here nothing is free. Cheerfulness always comes at the expense of somebody else.

For him the pain began at the very same moment she turned on the shower. Because drop by drop the water carried with it each one of the pawings in the movies, the scant success of his nightly caresses after those greasy suppers eaten in restaurants by the river. Josefina de la Puente bathed thoroughly after years of keeping corners of her body to herself, while Rogelio de la Puente's teeth were chattering with genital intensity. Rogelio had been spying on her through the window of the Institute ever since the ambulance took her there, and each one of her high notes in the shower brought him stinging pains, sharp aches and pangs that threw him into a frantic acrobatic dance.

How it stings you
how it screws you
don juan don juan
of the sole of my foot
red rogelio helio
helio
scratch if it itches
float away float away
my rogelio

Josefina went on singing, muddled and carefree in the shower. The astounded orderlies inside and the passers-by outside watched multicolored droplets land on Rogelio's white curls as he kept dancing his therapeutic dance, an attraction for both children and adults.

Success, like a shower

Certainly. Don't insist, my dear commercial-minded readers, taken in by the advertising claims and the urge to buy for yourselves the same pastries that Josefina had gorged on so happily. Of course. Immediately after the sirens they appeared, those types carrying laptops and cellular phones in their pockets, to say to Rogelio: We like your act and the droplets are enchanting. We find your dance charming and that flexing of the knees intriguing. Over and over we ask ourselves, how do you keep from breaking your neck? How can you keep up the rhythm without stopping even to take a pee? You have talent. You're gutsy and we'll make money, movies, do cabaret shows. Stop a few minutes. Come, we'll put you on TV. Your name is Rogelio? de la Puente?

**si por mar, en un buque de guerra /
si por tierra, en un tren militar . . .**

In the house next door, Adelita was thinking and almost said out loud:
—My dearest sweetheart, merciless arthritic, snatched treasure from the wrecks of passion: I've watched your attempts at arrogance to the point of madness, have let myself be carried along by your narcissistic imagination, but now it's time for us to make a visit in all seriousness to the boundless terrain of our modest old age. Dressed as a princess, I wait for you in the garden beside the grill.

And so they met, Adelita and Braulio, for the stroll that would take them through passageways of garlands and bibelots to the frontline of the war. They didn't expect the children in the orphanage to clap when they appeared nor could they deal properly with the soap bubbles escaping through Josefina's bathroom window as she sang an old Italian song she'd learned in the nuns' school.

They swallowed bubbles

Ended up as doormats

Rags for the floor

Some salvagable

Some losers mired in their own shit

I clutch you, knead you, leave you like new, massage you, put color into your veins, examine you, and make you whole again. What a serenade Miguel sang to Adelita. What slaps he gave her. Wake up, you old bitch, terror of impotent men, fantasy of beauty shops, witch, wake up, I'll rejuvenate, invigorate you and put some starch into you. Mantled in her own youth, Adelita rose up a heroine and sang a patriotic hymn so full of conviction and with such lyrics that Miguel was frightened, filled with resentment, furious, and with the strength only terror can provide said to her:

  Bye-bye

    Bye-bye

      till later

      till never

        I'm off to the dance
        I'm off to the club
        I'm off to the house of the Otherwoman
        so she'll knit me cozy winter sweaters and let me rest
I'm fond of my arthritis I'm a wreck I'm reclining sweetly on my own banks.

The Otherwoman has a mercantile bent but he doesn't have a clue

Yes, now to clean this hole. Hang out the clothes, start the stew, my hands sore from bleach. My belly growling from hunger. But I have to get everything ready. Everything arranged so when Miguel comes he'll see the house sparkling. **So he'll feel comfortable.**

So he'll be delighted

So he knows that here he can trim his toenails

I'LL GATHER UP THE CLIPPINGS AND PUT THEM IN A LITTLE BOX

I prove my love for him and I swallow everything without sugar coating because that's how much I love Miguel. That's how much I like his comings and goings, his way of changing my brain, the way he makes my heart beat faster, with the remote control always in his hand, searching for the TV program that will lull us into a stupor, make us sleep peacefully after the stew, the little glass of wine, a light dessert.

—Here I am to see you, my queen, my housewife, my nanny, my dearest love.

The Otherwoman is demure, asexual, her underclothes starched, her panties dry, spick-and-span; the Otherwoman loves him for real without ulterior motives or orgasmic sighs. Miguel is happy. Miguel looks unblinking into her eyes because now he knows they're united forever. He's eaten the doughnuts. Has belched, chewed, savored every bite down to the last carrot in the stew.

—My big hippopotamus, my baby. Let me smooth the calluses from your feet. Any buttons for me to sew on? My virtuoso lover. I approach with devotion. I lie by your side without touching you and sing lullabies so you'll think we had children who've already grown up and left the house.

For years this was the way Miguel recovered from his matrimonial excesses. Old spinster. Old spinster. Ugly butterball, the Otherwoman's neighbors would say. What did they know? Shitty gossips. Meanwhile she watered the plants on the balcony, taking a special interest in the progress of the flower shoots that bore those balloonlike flowers of bright vivid colors Miguel liked so much.

The Otherwoman worked like a dog. Her collection of clients grew enormously. Miguel three times a week, Rubén from time to time when there was a storm and he felt so much nostalgia for his mama. Carlos every time his fly bulged out and he longed for a world with nothing inconveniently sexy about it that would allow him to get his engineering degree and work out a future that would fit in with the plans of a country on the move. The Otherwoman, patriotic and mysterious, foresaw possibilities of profit, understood how one could reach fabulous objectives by remembering how forlorn men felt at having to provoke orgasmic sighs in wives and lovers; so, without fanfare or champagne, she opened the Academy. Rogelio, in spite of living next door, knew nothing about it till much later, much too late.

It's all a show from the start

When they drew the curtain, Antonia sighed and said: These guys need something heavy. Less posing and more dancing. Less dreaming and more rambunctious rampage. Too much observation and sentimentality. In that country the men ogled the women, all of them actresses. The men came to the theater, trousers somewhat wrinkled and seats worn from sitting in the office so much, and sank back in the cushy armchairs, but the women, vivacious live wires, screamed and yelled. The performances were excellent. Since there was no room for critics, the shows ended in furtive but frank pleasure. Until the children arrived.

They began by collecting trash: peacock feathers that Doña Francisca imported by mistake for the carnival that wound up in hisses and political campaigns, plaques, emblems, medals, charred wood in the sawmill sawdust of the beginning, crates of electronic gadgets suddenly forwarded by a nervous employee full of tics and acne, paintings acquired during the glory days. The rowdy kids appeared at teatime with tummies growling from hunger, eyes alert for advantages, and in two minutes won the all-out war against the cockroaches. They devoured, transformed, polished, and swallowed the garbage now speedily recycled, ready to be bread; GIRL FRIENDS BOY FRIENDS was a demolition company turned New Age restaurant, was, my dears, the conscience of a conservation-conscious age, ecological, but let's not fool ourselves, there wasn't an ounce of generosity in their bones. They lived for themselves; mirror in hand, they licked their lips and made videos of themselves kicking the neighbor. That was their idea of love, these children ready for anything, forgetful but always in motion and active, little aerobic bodies, mamas' treasures at times, pitiless tyrants at others.

Now you know why the women didn't pay too much attention to the play. They were totally preoccupied by the fate of that infantile devouring army. They never knew whether to grab the kids by the ear, force them to do their lessons: Baby, don't put your hands in the garbage, come here so I can cut your nails. They said: What's the use of insisting on good manners and handwriting if they're going to roll around in shit and build things from it? Better to forget about them or even if you do keep one eye on them be sure to have the papers and birth certificates handy in case they should change their habits one day and decide to go live abroad or become engineers or perhaps even better set up an ice cream stand on one of the broad streets of the neighborhood just beneath a balcony with a glistening rubber tree on the left that dripped on rainy days and ruined the hairdo of some woman who was still teasing her hair, poor thing, where's she been during the last twenty years of *Vogue?* the pretty girls were thinking to themselves, outside the Institute, free, independent, comediennes, most of them divas on alternate weekends.

. . . loving you is my punishment

They ate grapes. Lay in a hammock, and while Josefina tried to keep her balance, Rogelio lifted up her dress to enter the cavernous city of her fuzz, pushed its limits, articulated a humid damp music she could hear only with eyes closed. For love she was always a bit catatonic. Acted like a dead woman in bed but was as loudmouthed as a politician when jealous. Rogelio went searching for the mouth of her vagina, wanted it to speak to him, begged it, asked it for a story, an insult, a name, but Josefina kept the secret of her city with an anguished silence throughout the thirty-six years of a marriage consummated every night and during many siestas.

Mute woman. Sleepwalker. The one with the confirmation dress with red dots. The virgin of the procession. The statue of a woman who suddenly believes she's not made of marble, runs to take a pee and returns immediately to the pedestal without anyone noticing. A nurse with a mask who laughs out loud in the middle of a serious operation. Rogelio chose an image and fucked it on Josefina's body, reached ecstasy alone, shook her, hoped to have reached her, but Josefina, proud, turned over and went to sleep. They were happy because the house was in order, because they greeted the neighbors with a smile, because they had two perfect children who were graduates of the military academy, and because Josefina always sang while making meat balls.

they come in pairs; do you think they do everything together?

During the earliest days of her marriage, Antonia was extremely anxious, wanting to talk constantly with the woman next door. The minute she saw her neighbor come home from work she was out to greet her and say, How are you? What's happened with the story of the boss and the secretary? What color is in style these days in the offices in the city? Have you heard any political rumors? Josefina brought her news of a bureaucratic and mysterious world. To work in a government office, a ministry, was Antonia's greatest dream as she spent her day cleaning and scrubbing and watching soap operas. Josefina, with her high heels and proud bearing, would say:

we refused that worthless bitch because the file was incomplete

and the other one because she forgot to put an accent mark in her aunt's surname, and I said to her very sternly, "Do you believe we're some sort of jackasses here, some screwed-up nobodies, we understand very well that such a document can be extremely valuable, extremely valuable, and we're not going to hand it out to just any forger." Let her come back tomorrow, bring the aunt with the birth certificate notarized by three authorities and with all the requisite seals. Let them wait in line. I'm not one to give things away just like that.

And she sighed as she kicked off her shoes, and Antonia watched as her feet swelled, her bunions bulged, and the room filled with a scent that was so wholly her own and yet with such an officelike aura that spoke of paper on her feet, a message of cigarettes, coffee cups, good networking.

After the first few months of conversations, Antonia began to get more peppy and suggested that Josefina take a long bath at her house. Look at all this bubble bath, it belongs to the kids, but it doesn't matter, I'll get some more tomorrow. Lying in the tub, Josefina drank chocolate milk and told story after story of her stubborn refusals, imitated the smile she put on when she turned desperate petitioners away, making Antonia feel utterly happy and successful because to her Josefina said yes, accepted her chocolate milk, her bubble bath, her bathtub, let her sit beside her, soap her back and watch her, as resplendent as maría félix, a real woman, the way movie stars were when a body could still be shocking.

Rogelio and Alberto would meet at noon in a bar around the corner from the racetrack. They'd check the results of their bets and divide winnings. Alberto, his head like an egg, his tiny eyes half-closed, would calculate the figures out loud with a lisp that put Rogelio's nerves on edge. With thixty-two maketh theven thixty and thix thousand, not tho bad. And your part cometh to theven hundred and thixty. Whatcha thay, big guy? Thay thomething, thilly boy. Rogelio took the bills, hitched up his pants, tried not to look at Alberto so people wouldn't confuse them, then made a move to go. No, big boy, you thtay right here. We'll eat a thteak to thelebrate, don't leave me alone with tho much loot, thuch a windfall courtethy of lady luck. The wine and the steak, what a melody for the innards. They became best friends again every time they won, congratulated each other, hatched plans to leave their wives and go off to live on a south sea island where they could have well-turned-out broads, bet it all in one night and come out on top, winners, act like foreigners strolling along a tropical street where people sweat even when wearing the thinnest of shirts and bright-colored shorts, to walk, walk along cobbled streets, following a barefoot woman who turns around and winks an eye.

When they got to that part, Alberto scratched his bald head lasciviously and announced that he probably wouldn't follow her, that she'd end up being just like his wife. The very thame ath Elena. Don't you underthtand? They're all the thame. They thay come with me, take off my thlippers, come with me, but then lead you thtraight to the kitchen tho you'll thet them up in an apartment and thtay to play gameth with the kidth. Enough of following girlth, big boy. But Rogelio continued to follow her in his dreams, in his office as he checked the files. He followed her until she came to a door where she smiled, waved good-bye, and vanished before turning the doorknob. Thanks to her Rogelio led a methodical life, bought presents for Josefina, preened before the mirror, and counted gray hairs with the contemplative dignity of an anchorite.

Oh, if only you could've seen Elena after Alberto left. The rushing around. The joy of her small behind being poured into tight jeans. Powder on the cheeks. Lots of rouge. And running shoes to get there fast. Before anybody else. How are you today. How did you sleep and what did they give you to eat. What may I do for you. So very friendly. Respected, admired. She knelt down, gave one a massage and went on to the next. I'll put a compress on your forehead to lower the fever. I'll give you your medication. Quick because I have to go. Pick up the check and leave. Elena finished her job in the geriatric ward and in two minutes, dressed as a fortuneteller, eyes widened by kohl, striking mole on the chin and her very mouth now colored by premonitions, settled in the booth. The fortunes she predicted moved her to tears. The future was an island where lost children found the tenderest of mothers and gentle old ladies danced in dimmed light with lubricious adolescent sweethearts, politicians made endless speeches before ecstatic crowds, and she received her women friends in a mansion filled with chocolates and mirrors. Until Rogelio turned up, angry. I want the barefoot woman. I want her to open the door and I don't want her to vanish. Give me some advice. Something practical. Not hope. I don't want hope. That's for jerk-offs. Just the barefoot woman to talk with me about whatever she wants. Elena recognized him right away and beneath the kohl of her eyes scrutinized the de Puente marriage, compared it with her own, and asked herself: Where does he get the money to pay me if Josefina doesn't even have enough to buy kohl?

like always somebody is plotting, counting money, selling fortunes

—My feet are cold. It doesn't seem possible that with all we spend on heat they haven't managed to get this place warm. There's no reason for it. They're a bunch of imbeciles. Bring the foreman and have him shot. We'll accuse him of treason, of collaborating with the enemy. Better yet, embezzlement of funds. With that you're never far from the truth in any case. I'm so furious and so cold.
—It's because marble is not only expensive but cold. I think that's why they use it in dairies. So the merchandise doesn't get ruined. I for one like this building with the high ceilings and black-and-white floors. I feel a person can do anything, and the people who come in seem so small, I mean in size. But we, sitting on this rostrum and wearing our boots, gain height and prestige. After all, they didn't do too bad a job with the architecture. We're the way we are. It's a building for wearing boots.
—Shh. I hear footsteps. They must be bringing in the accused women. Let's get our boots back on. Wipe your mouth. You dribbled chocolate.

They brought them in a group, pale, untidy, in gray uniforms and slippers. Some came hunched over so as not to show their breasts, others covered the pelvis. They'd been dressed for such a long time that the clothing seemed to have no weight and all their gestures had been adapted to a manufactured nudity. Every one exactly like the next, and on the faces not a trace of the makeup that used to distinguish them from one another. The director looked at them as if he could actually see them and said aloud: Ugly, tall, short, too fat, and too thin. All unsightly, I accuse you and do not absolve you. Three hundred and fifty-five awful women caught last month in different parts of the city.

Contemptuous women who disregard the role they should fulfill in order to keep the energy level of the machos of the country at peak capacity.

Frigid women and lesbians.

Women absorbed by vague, uncommunicable ideas, devoid of flirtatious ways. Unappetizing women who never learned how to cook and don't want to offer a little warmth.
Sterile women
good-for-nothings
spineless
I accuse you and at this moment condemn you to work in the Institute, to clean, make pastries for patriotic holidays, mend clothes, look for the needle in the haystack. You are never to look us in the face if we do not order you to do so.

While the director was speaking, the women all together began scratching their left elbows and the scrraff-scrraff of their nails against the cloth made a disconcerting little tune that warmed their feet and their souls. The director and the deputy director both took it as proof of more guilt, making them feel unselfish and good about themselves. They said: If you wish, you may roll up your sleeves, but after a brief silence the women suddenly whirled and left through the enormous open doors to go to their corners, leaving a trail of piss that tinted the marble yellow. While the piss ran down through the grate constructed for that purpose, the director and the deputy director congratulated themselves on the good quality of their boots and took the inventory they had to turn in with a report to the inspector general. They always lied, disguised numbers with zeros, subtracted and added phoney surgical procedures and treatments for the condemned, dreamt up specialized and enormously expensive diets, granted phantom rooming houses to relatives killed in the War of Independence, made sure that the most prestigious hairdressers of the city signed invoices for oddball treatments to prevent and provoke baldness or cure dandruff of the eyelashes, and added recommendations for pedicures to cure red, green, and yellow blisters. A task that required anxious days and nights. They gave free rein to their imagination suitable for CPAs while working in that luxurious corner that always offered the same alternatives: in the winter blasts of air or the urine smell that pierced their bones like a stiletto, and in the summer mosquitos, flies, bloodsuckers, or the piss now insolent, heavy, swirling around in their heads, on their foreheads, burning in their nostrils. They all suffered from chronic sinusitis.

the condemned women

Josefina de la Puente came in a littleoldlady but did not lose her bent for spirited hijinks. They took her in for being ugly, obscene, for having forgotten about Rogelio, for not reacting to him when he spied on her through the window of her own house. She had lost her memory to such an extreme that she no longer showed signs of having lived, moved like a baby, drank milk constantly, and stole candy from her neighbors. But now she was singing new songs and her repertory kept receding further and further into the past. She started with the vaudeville tunes her mother, while pregnant, had heard in the theater every night before doing her striptease act. Josefina imagined herself blissful in the fetal position, as her mother bawled those songs in bad French because Yvonne had given up her mother tongue the first month her period was late and used it only for her work in dimly lit rooms where sailors brought foreign perfumes and paid more for the wine when it was served by a woman with an accent from the other side of the ocean, and she also began to croon zarzuelas telling of fleeting love misadventures sung by her grandmother in Almería. Rosa was the first to call her the radio woman and Josefina became the condemned women's delight. They sat her down and with a little milk and some affectionate pats a quick postmenopausal festival would get under way, a tribute to Yvonne and to Rosa though they never got along well in life but now, in Josefina's amnesia, they sang as a duet, brilliant, almost divas.

Rosa, Filomena, and Rebeca were teenagers. The three of them had been rounded up after a high school phys. ed. class. Caught on a bus, wearing no make-up, braces on their teeth, and smelling sweaty. Enough to arouse the indignation of an agent who made them get off immediately and called the patrol car. They didn't find it difficult to adjust. They could talk for hours about their romantic exploits, totally ignoring the clumsy little sweethearts that served as pretext for their conversations, and instead of plotting to run away from their homes they concentrated on exploring the walls of the institution, stealing records of the youngest condemned and changing the numbers the authorities had invented with so much effort. A real army on the move, they were preparing almost casually for a revolution with no concern for the outcome. They chewed gum smuggled in by Rogelio's agent, who wanted to get Josefina out at night so she could appear with him in his act. Rebeca had promised him she would get Josefina out some night wrapped in a blanket but until then he must keep her supplied with chewing gum, cookies, sanitary napkins, and photos of rock stars. The agent brought everything they asked for because he was an honest man and dreamed of lifting his family out of poverty by means of the extraordinary show featuring the amnesiac couple; years and years of working in the ministry had taught him that sweet-smelling breath got you nowhere and neither did wearing jacket and tie; you had to find a shortcut, an attractive and practical idea, one that made it easier to get up every day and go through the routine. He was preparing for the amnesiac couple's act gladly but without hurry, diligently, and with his shoes well polished.

branded forever in my soul

He had not forgotten her. His face became sad and his heart beat faster whenever he thought of her. In the middle of the circus he leapt up and began to dance with jerky movements, on purpose to astound the onlookers, particularly the girl with golden curls and teeth darkened by too much insecticide in the toothpaste in common use again during the last two years of the epidemic, and he also wanted to impress the priest who blew his nose, sounding like a train whistle, every time Rogelio landed safe and sound and balanced himself on the big toe of his left foot, but actually Rogelio was back at the dance celebrating Josefina's fifteenth birthday. He courted her by the minty gum held discreetly in his mouth and cologne that penetrated Josefina's stiffness in his arms and made her sigh. Then he'd hold her tighter, only to pull back to let the gap between them cool down so she'd be the one to close the distance and lean against him, her dress, already wrinkled, grazing his fly. He courted the absent-minded woman and pretended amnesia so the agent would bring her out, earned modest tips accumulating in the tent ready for whatever bribes might be required. Because at bottom as well as on top Josefina was the carrier of the sap, the atmosphere of his youth, Rogelio longed for the refuge of her voice, to eat once again in her kitchen, smell the passage of time between her legs.

Dear disenchanted, undeceived, skeptical friends: this love was like any other, and in that city of vendors, speculators, genuflecting bureaucrats, Rogelio's erections ended in a melancholy milk that stained the slacks he wore for dancing.

The girl with the golden curls clicked her tongue. Enough. I've flattered him enough. Time to get acquainted; stop trying to corral him. This man's got talent and he owes me something.

—Good evening. I've been watching you for some time, and if you allow me, I would like to tell you that your act gladdens my life. Even the treatment for my teeth seems to be more effective since I've been coming to watch you. But you're missing something, you

dance like a crazed man with two left feet because you've lost someone. I warn you and assure you that
   I don't come looking for confidences
   I don't want to tell you a story the same as your own
   I don't need your pity
   I don't intend to show you any signs of affection
—But you are just a little girl.
—Clearly your eyesight is not good! It's the curls I fix each morning when I get out of bed. It's the cream I just bought in the drugstore. It's the dose of rejuvenating chocolate I take after each meal. It's the tape with flirtatious come-ons I listen to before going out in the street.
—Rogelio de la Puente, delighted
—Camila
—Camila . . .
—Camila. Don't be so formal, we're in the circus.
—I have a business proposition that could fill up your free hours of the morning. I need a portrait artist. I want my family to be resurrected from the past. I'll talk to you, tell you, describe them, and your job is to embody them, imitate them, and make them walk through my house.
—That'll be expensive, you know. A reconstruction job like that.
—I know that already; if I wanted to do it cheap, I'd go to the movies. But on the other hand, my friend, you're down on your luck, you're missing something. No. Don't tell me what it is. I don't want to start feeling sorry for you and have you ask me for a raise. Never, OK? Never that sort of thing. Little secrets, intimacy. None of that.
—Better that way.
—I'll be the one to tell things but I don't ever wish to know about you because in this matter there should be no confusion whatever.

★ ★ ★

At that moment Rogelio felt an irresistible desire to shout and Camila was not afraid when with a big laugh he began to muss up her curls to see for himself, to judge and leave her breathless.

(we should have a sparkling woman lawyer, just in case)

She was in a hurry. Two clients had cancelled their afternoon appointments and she'd decided to go to work for the condemned women. It's very important for a female lawyer to perform free and difficult services. It lends prestige. Gives a boost to the career. Makes you into a personality on the social scene and later you can parlay the experience into something else. Marisa was bent on not letting one minute of her young years go by without profiting. Time later for wrinkles, a comfortable house near the ocean, and perhaps an unassuming widower who would enjoy going with her to the theater. Count her money in the bank. For now, build up stock, make something out of herself. She no longer slept since the pharmacies now imported the elixir and the nights simply perched atop the mornings, resulting in marvels of productivity. Each day more highly esteemed, always in demand, always in a hurry.

She arrived at the clinic out of breath but with eyes wide open and shining, gleaming from the elixir with the greenness that now marked a generation of go-getting professionals.

—Priceless Marisa, always in time to resolve a crisis.

—Thank you very much, Mr. Director.

—Would it be too much trouble for you to give me an opinion regarding a recently condemned woman? I would like to know if the circumstances of her apprehension are in accordance with the existing law. It's the first time that someone we wished to punish developed an attitude of complacency, a state of mind that seems to make a joke of our punitive measures, thereby putting the entire system at risk. Here are the papers. Josefina de la Puente. They call her the radio woman.

Marisa sat down near the grill and the constant reek of urine brought on a minor allergic reaction. The elixir did not mix well with urine, since it worked in direct contradiction to human physiology and violently disrupted natural rhythms, but Marisa, by now used to her wheezes, simply knit her brow and read: **Admitted as old woman, develops amnesia, and believes she is a baby.**

got to go / don't ask me where or why

I can't hang out the clothes or iron your shirts. Even though it may take only five and a half minutes, even though in fact I would enjoy the acrobatics around the ironing board, the circling of the clothes in the centrifuge, the texture of the cotton when I starch your cuffs. I can't cook the stew, the one that made us warble with joy, and it's not because I don't want to drink the wine we keep in the cupboard or because it bothers me to fry the onions and add a few red peppers with minced garlic. I can't make the bed, wax the floor, clean the soap scum from the bath tub until the porcelain shines like new and we feel we're lovers, lustful, agree to the massage with rejuvenating creams and warm our feet beneath the flowered sheets my aunt gave us, the one who lives in the country. I have urgent messages, two or three glances I received in the street and could not return during the last few years, I must ponder a certain dream. I'm on a bicycle, wearing only a black garter belt, and a girl jumping rope comes up and invites me to a snack of cookies and milk. It bothers me, annoys me that I'm missing the taste of that snack in my stomach, it's essential that I go and find a bench in the square where someone I do not know is saving a place for me so together we can weave a conversation in a language that escapes me at the moment. Bye.

I should tell you that Roberto was surprised. The toothpick that seemed to be solidly ensconced between a molar and the remains of a pizza he had eaten after seeing his last patient fell out of his mouth, his feet and hands suddenly grew cold, and he concluded that an empty feeling would always be with him until the moment when he could once again sit with Clara on a bench in the square and become the person she'd find by chance on some mild afternoon when financial circumstances were favorable for the country, and then they'd end by embracing each other in a ballroom where a cotillion celebrating a fifteen-year-old's birthday was under way with shiny candies in semitropical colors trampled on the floor.

That's why he began to learn foreign languages, bought a young tourist's gear, got a camera, and went about the city memorizing bits of conversation in Russian, Hungarian, medieval Latin, Quechua, and also Lunfardo. He found some moments in his classes exciting as when an Indian girl just arrived from Toluca immediately grasped the English system of accentuation and with unnatural speed asked for white tea and sandwiches. The memory of Clara was a vernacular illusion and each time Roberto stumbled in the conjugations he imagined her silent, approving his efforts, her face lit by signs, almost a dictionary.

Get ready, darlings. Like the ugly women you should be meticulous, neat, imaginative, and above all insultingly clean.

The girls paraded for the other internees in military formation. They had organized their troops according to their birth or anticipated death dates. Young ones attracted by the vertigo of the window, the weight of their own bodies falling onto the sidewalk, the warm blood spurting from the veins, and the scene of the grief-stricken family in the cemetery mingled with old ladies with arteriosclerosis and skeptical women miserable from migraines, premenstrual acne, backaches. An army with nothing to lose. The agents believed they could humiliate them by putting them in jail for being ugly but the women were thinking of other things. Gleefully they told how they'd managed to get themselves arrested, the tricks they'd used to attract the attention of absent-minded agents in a fierce sharp struggle by faking defects, tics, cavities, wrinkles. So when the girls began to get organized, a feeling of euphoria permeated the recruits' physiology. They had to make an effort to keep that air of hopelessness they wore in the institution and only behind the authorities' backs did they let their glittering smiles really gleam, the pride of their lithe erect bodies.

—My husband came to complain. I saw him the other evening with a briefcase full of documents.

—None of the documents are worth anything. If they see you, they see you and they grab you.

—But he came with the pictures, the ones they took of us nude. It was a joke, our friends said, so we could all feel like movie stars and the truth is I liked it although if I'd known ahead of time I wouldn't have eaten meatballs just an hour before because they bloat you so, but now perhaps it might work, to prove we really enjoyed ourselves in bed. How I trusted him, you know? A woman who lets those things be done to her is a woman guys like and when they realize I'll do anything they want they'll let me go and come as I please. I can wear make-up and a cheerful face day and night, go from shower to toilet without a word being said.

—And why go back to your house?

—María, you're so out of it. You don't notice anything. I adore my television programs, I like my work as international telephone operator. I get a kick out of the beep-beep of calls from new zealand, hong kong, mar del plata. Every Sunday a priest calls a boy who's his son, he says, and asks for money to pay for a ticket so he can come and visit but the boy says the priest is not his father, that it's a well-known trick and to stop annoying him, but the priest keeps calling collect and although the ungrateful son complained to the company I put the calls through. Let him pay. If he doesn't want to send travel money to the poor old guy, let him pay and be annoyed. The funniest thing was when he came to the office with a guy he passed off as his real father. And my supervisor was there and said to him: Look, I'm not interested in who or what this gentleman is that you've just introduced to me here, you talk as if we had time to verify who's calling, to find out about what's going on. To you your life may be very interesting, but we are professionals and very busy. You should see the number of permits we process every day. If you don't want to pay, don't and arrange the matter with the judge, get a lawyer. Please, sir, don't mess up the counter with that pastry, the sugar sticks to the papers. **Next please**. And that thrilled me, that **Next please**. You can't imagine how marvelous it is. And later were the old ladies, subscribers to the line of broken engagements. They telephone to any bordering country and are put in contact with a man who tells them he's dying of love for them. He tells them how much he misses them, gives them details: When I talk to you I remember how we held hands before going into the hallway of your house and then I can't stand it any longer and right now I'm unzipping my fly very slowly like I used to do so you wouldn't notice and suddenly you found yourself with me pointing directly at your cunt and everything was easy because it was hot and you found it more comfortable to go without panties I miss you and can't hold out any longer, tell me how much you love me because I feel I can't

go on like this come to see me and I'll show you what I feel for you.
—And isn't there a woman who wants to go?
—No. They know it's a hoax. Besides, they're all retired and the cost of the call alone leaves them with little to eat on; to travel across the border would cost them a bundle on top of the cost of health insurance and all the rest, the eye exam, the reciting of multiplication tables, but occasionally there's one who digs in her heels, forgets she's paid for the service and goes nuts. But there'd been no problem till last week. As it happens, one of the old ladies won the lottery and now wants to visit her telephone sweetheart. She knows he's working for the Engagements of Yesteryear Company but it doesn't matter to her and, María, I'm dying of curiosity and instead am shut up here, plotting for who knows what.
—Clever us, because we can help you escape, Tota, and if you get your job back we could use you to plan our actions in the city. Clever. Clever. Clever. Clever. I love the rhythm. Let's see, dance with me. Like this. As if it were your adoring sweetheart of yesteryear. Clever. Clever. Clever. A little forward thrust of the waist, here we go.   Clever, clever, clever, swinging operator. I saw you lick your lips and get all worked up when you were telling about the last call. Look at you, you dance as if you knew.

bloodsucker

She strolls by herself as if she were levitating. She just passed a movie theater and it never occurred to her to go in. A guy followed her down the street making suggestions about beds, sheets, or if not a dark corner or a café or just a glass of wine but it made no impression. She walks alone and goes into a house with half-drawn curtains where a boy seated at the piano is playing an indefinable composition. They recognize one another. She kisses him on the forehead and goes to the kitchen to prepare a complicated meal with vaguely nutritious steaming liquids.

—Did everything go all right for you at school today?

—The teacher hates me. Today she made me leave the room because she thinks I make fun of her; she says I make myself look like a ghost on purpose.

—She's afraid of you. Nobody likes kids who are too bright. Don't worry about it. It's true the kid is thin and there's something dark and haunting in the circles under his eyes, but she smiles at him and chatters away about anything because it's getting late and she doesn't want the members of the group to criticize her again. Only fifteen minutes till the uncle arrives to take care of his nephew as he does every night. Fifteen minutes turn into twenty but now the doorbell is ringing.

—Sorry to be late but here I am with my tongue hanging out because I know my little nephew is waiting for me and I can't fail to be here.

She already has her bag prepared and with a smile the boy cannot see says: I'll be back at the usual time, like always, thank you, many thanks, good night, enjoy yourselves. The uncle is so excited his mouth is watering. The boy is used to it although at times he chooses to think of other things. A birthday, the boat he saw in the pond in the park, the blue stripe in his white socks. Her name is Teresa Jiménez and she's a manicurist. In the garage where he works the uncle is known as Rafa and nobody remembers the name of the boy since he died a few months later and memory of him vanished along with the house and the sound of the piece he played that at bottom didn't even interest Clara, his piano teacher.

when the service is free, you never know what to expect

—I'm Dr. Marisa Format and I've come to ask you a few questions to see if we might make some progress in your case.
—How much blood are you going to draw from me? Look, I don't care what you use it for but after these sessions my voice is very weak, and there's no way I can put up with that. Because here I crackle like a castanet, as you can plainly see. I dance, I sing, I keep myself company, and without a mirror I enjoy myself. So if you're thinking of blood, dear Doctor Marisa Format, forget it, because from now on I'll give you test tubes with grenadine, none of my own frisky fresh blood that keeps me artistic, joking, a delight for my companions, the internees. Or better yet, I'll grab the syringe and draw some of your blood, Marisita, because you seem a bit dull to me in any case. Didn't anybody ever tell you how insipid you look? Of course, nobody ever says anything to women doctors because they're seen as filled with abnegation, in the lab day and night with the skeletons and the formaldehyde, so many years of study, but I'm sure that half the time is spent screwing with the ones who hand out the diplomas. Because I've seen everything in this world. How many deals I've missed out on, but now I'm here and that's it, understand? Marisita, about the business of the blood. If you want blood, draw some of your own since it seems to me you would still be menstruating. Oh, no, no, wait. What red eyes! And that tic! You must be one of those rich enough to afford the elixir. Tell me . . .
—Señora de la Puente, I'm a lawyer not a medical doctor and I'm not here to take your blood. I'm volunteering my services at this Institute to make sure that you internees are treated properly and to facilitate the return to the outside for those who so wish. I'd like to help you, stop scratching your elbow. Does your stomach hurt, is that why you keep twisting around that way?
—No, my dear, I love to have all my body close to my belly button. Talk, keep talking, I'm listening while I amuse myself:
    dear child of the elixir

>   wake up wake up little rosebud
>   the littlebitty girl
>   with skin like fried potatoes
>   eyes wide open from the elixir

Josefina's ditty lulled Marisa, and for the first time in five years she managed to rest her eyes, fixing them on Josefina's bared navel. Josefina rocked as she sang and Marisa felt a sudden thirst for milk that made her open her mouth and click her tongue.

—Dirty old sow. Pull your dress down immediately. Go to your corner, you make us guards sick. Excuse me, Dr. Format, but you never know with the internees and this one's a hopeless case. Just lucky we were passing through on our tour of inspection. You're not going to spend your time and care on an old sow like her, I don't know what gets into her to make her do these filthy things, because on top of everything else she has a terrific singing voice. What shall we do? Go to the next case or are you off to your office now?

a woman always has to be there for her man and so on and so forth

Clara walks down a stony road and sees that she has reached one of the predetermined places. A man with a thin moustache opens the door of a modest house, low ceilings, windows without curtains, and asks her to take off her muddy shoes before coming in. The doormat is somewhat damp from the rain, her feet hurt, and she could have stayed just like that enjoying the softness, the dampness oozing between her toes, but the other man is urging her to hurry, the session is about to begin. They'd been waiting hours for her. Clara apologizes and sees her chair is the one with garish colors beside an urn with oriental motifs.

—My name is Juan, my dear. They notified us two months ago and I was afraid you'd changed your mind.

—Be quiet, Juan. This is not the time for recriminations. If Clarita needs anything, ask Ramón who's here to serve her.

—Girl, you can begin, get up on the table and just begin, we're watching you.

—Like this, without music?

—She wants music, music, next she'll want a curtain and a sweetheart and an engagement ring

    next she wants a fifteenth-birthday party

    next she'll want me

    to take a shower

        put on clean socks

        blow soap bubbles at her

    music a little music for the little miss

stop screwing around, there're only the three of us, get started and later if we like you we'll make it sweet.

—No, no, no, and no. Don't take off your blouse that way. First you blow us a little kiss. Look, I'll show you how. And put your hand at your waist. Let's see how you swing it. Look at Juan, how he wiggles his waist. That's it, my king. Now your turn, Clarita, don't you see it's better without music? I'll blow in your ear and tickle you here and there. Seems hard to believe that a first-class entertainer would have that sort of underwear. In your place, I'd buy myself things of the highest quality. In your place, I'd give you some ass, Juan.

Clara's life in that house was pure paradise. Day and night she practiced an extravagant silent striptease. Juan and Ramón coupled with great enthusiasm during her performances. They gave her detailed and ferocious lessons and let her satisfy herself alone, excited, before the mirror, legs apart, hand curious.

—My best student.
—Not the prettiest.
—And not the ugliest.
—What lack of elegance.
—It's not elegance. It's purchasing power.
—Let her go out and earn her own bread.
—We're tired, Clara.
—We don't like broads up down or sideways.
—Once you've learned you're no longer amusing.
—You two are old, you don't enjoy yourselves because you don't really know the score. A dining table, miserable meals, office routine, and me as your student, although this I tell you out of pure spite because I'm in love with you both, don't throw me out, I'll work at anything, I'll get into high schools incognito to find boys for you, I'll rob banks and the three of us will go on a cruise over blue waters with disney-like little fish, I'll seduce the girl next door and we'll put on a number that will give you extravagant erections, from now on I'll do the cooking, I never told you but I know how to make roast turkey with glazed potatoes I put sugar on them just before they begin to brown every Sunday I'll make it every Sunday or every day if you wish and this time when you get up I'll give you a foot massage no kidding and if your feet are dirty I'll wash them myself but let me stay here because I'm in love with you dear fast lifetime friends.

Like you, I'm sad things had to turn out the way they did. Clara left, determined to carve out a competitive love life for herself, but it was very difficult at first because Juan and Ramón lived in a remote place and to get into the city she had to take various trains and buses full of short squatty men in dark clothes who without meaning to rubbed against her and were upset when she responded with touches so early in the morning, after all they'd barely emerged from their own beds, so they put her off the bus and shouted insults at her because they believed she was sent on purpose, a swindler who was out to infect them with the epidemic above all they were afraid of the clothing she wore so dirty because of the dusty road she might already be infected now she definitely seemed someone to be afraid of with her outfits too heavy for the season and her eyes drooping but she was in a constant state of excitement because she'd not yet forgotten Juan and Ramón and every leg that grazed hers reminded her of the dances, her intense apprenticeship in the house with the low ceilings.

with blood, without sweat, with tears

Elena had foreseen the birth of a baby girl in that city, one with curly, somewhat reddish hair, who at first glimpse of her mama would give her a slap after winking an eye at the surgeon, but she'd forgotten her own prediction until they carried her to the hospital, face red, feet swollen.

—Terrible that you wear such tight jeans as pregnant as you are.
—A miracle she's only fainted.
—The baby is going to come out like a candy cane.
—She might not even know that she was expecting.
—This one doesn't slow down for anything. I see her go from the Institute to the booth, change, and put on the airs of a fortuneteller. She's a cheat who works fast.
—But with children you can't do it.
—Nine months.
—Or seven.
—Who knows, maybe with fortunetellers it's different.
—Elena, her name is Elena, it says so on her bracelet.

That Cesarean was like no other. Quick. But expandable. Amanda came out like they had said, a kind of damp candy cane with curly red hair. It was her slap that woke Elena and not the screechy little voice that said: Must be my mama 'cause she's crying so hard, thanks Mr. Surgeon for opening the door for me.

2
I don't know why there always has to be war, why, since we're wounded already

Here they are: quite a little cabal sitting around in the basement of the Institute, drinking beer smuggled in the night before. The initial group has grown and now they need a leader, a woman capable of steering them in some direction. They don't know where. They just want to get somewhere the minute they can put together a complete sentence; their conversations consist of whispers, gasps of jokes, advice on how to fall asleep, how to soften calluses. If they were talking out loud, nobody would hear them because today there's a party going on upstairs: the director and the deputy director are celebrating their first decade of service to the country and the plotters in the basement would love to go up and take a collective and celebratory piss but they are dehydrated. They'll have to wait till tomorrow, after breakfast, but by then it'll be too late to create a real uproar. And then she arrived.

—It makes me sad to see your faces without make-up.
> So shining clean

Pimples in plain sight
> Innocent

Idle lambs
> Let's surprise them

Let's take the helm

And to prove she was a resourceful person, she opened her fist to reveal red nails as she tossed out round-trip tickets that fell among them now aroused from their deep lethargy.

—A while ago I could have been taken for one of you and look at me now.

They observed her as best they could but they'd forgotten how to judge; what they saw was merely informative despite the fact that they could see perfectly well her black velvet dress, the white skin decorated with blue tattoos made to look like veins showing hunting scenes, her shiny high-heeled boots, not the rubber ones the Institute personnel wore but patent leather; they noted the rhinestone earrings, the brooch, the beads, the bracelets, and a little

golden bell around her left ankle, and when she saw that still none of it made any impression on them, she took out a stole of live skunks and let them lick her neck. Raquel was the first to react, saying: What do these creatures eat? Will you lend them to me? Marina insisted on touching them and the skunks unwound themselves from around the woman's neck and began to run around the room while the internees in a hilarious chase started giving them names and nicknames: Here comes little butterball, lollypop, don't run away, look there goes dummy. They felt so good they tumbled over the basement floor with truly aerobic energy, ignoring both the rough places and the skunk shit now building up in bigger and bigger green-black piles when suddenly one of the skunks tried to hide behind the thin heel of the woman's boot, causing her to trip; the girls were knocked breathless because the velvet dress tied sarong fashion was torn off and what they saw was the thin hairy body of Braulio, who introduced himself this way:
—I wanted to get ahead in life. Earn a bit of money for my sick children. Better the circumstances of my family in this era of inflation and speculators . . .
—Interrogation! Interrogation! Stop talking nonsense.
    Enough speeches
        Enough fairy tales
            Interrogation
we demand an interrogation with all that the law allows, we'll get the syringes ready, the files of information, here's the cot, what luck we're in the basement, we'll carry out our interrogation and keep careful notes.
—But if that's exactly what I say to you, enough speeches, I'm telling you the truth and that's that.
—This one doesn't understand anything, he doesn't even know what an interrogation is, we have to hurry because when the people

upstairs find out what happened we all have to be in bed. What if we just take him with us to the ward?

They called him The Infiltrator. Braulio didn't care because when he took on the job of spying on them he was already tired of his seesaw marriage and of working so hard to pay for the sessions at the Academy, to say nothing of the tensions in the convent where the neurotic little nuns would've ended by grabbing and fucking him at the most unexpected moment, and now he enjoyed working for a group of women who had no interest in him, who didn't watch his every move or demand that he say a rosary every night in a schoolgirl singsong. Occasionally he felt very frustrated remembering moments of his adolescence when he knew who was who and the world was divided between pricks and cunts, so when a committee of girls informed him of the mission they required him to take on—to act as Tota's boyfriend, go around with her, take care of her: Help us so she can escape; chat with the authorities while we arrange her getaway; make sure her job as telephone operator comes through without a hitch so we can have contact with the outside—Braulio felt as excited as a young man and agreed but hid his glee so the girls wouldn't catch on to how enthusiastic he was and would leave him alone again to tend to the skunks, who'd turned into demanding and capricious pets.

it's smuggled? I'll take a dozen

With great aplomb he walked back and forth through the airport. At every corner he knew somebody who took care of baggage, packages, or tickets. A wink of the eye this way and that and he could smuggle anything in. And what with one thing and another I shouldn't have to explain more to you, because at some time we've all seen how it works and have even bought, sold, wanted, compared prices and goods, but the little girl with the camera hadn't known she shouldn't take pictures and followed him all over, won over by the way he walked, so very straight, with the tightfitting jacket and those shining loafers, his raw-silk tie intrigued her, and above all she wanted him to pose with her, proof to her girlfriends that she'd been in a real international airport with men dressed to kill in incredible styles but absolutely essential for an up-and-coming country.

—Girl, stop following me. One picture is enough. Where are your parents?

—Don't be such an old fart, mine have provided me with plenty of goodies, they've sent me to all the expensive private schools and fed me the elixir since I was born, now I don't need them, I have a doctorate in literature and I do photography because I haven't yet found a way to become a tourist, I suppose I'll have to become a *femme fatale* or something like that but since I'm only ten years old the candidates run from me because they don't understand, you know?

—Ten years old . . .

—You too, so much running around, so much persuading with the looks and the clothes but there's no point, ten years with the elixir multiply, expand; while the others sleep, we privileged ones grow in the dark, prowl with cats, measure the heartbeat of caterpillars, spy on cockroaches, and save ourselves all sorts of silliness.

—Would you like to buy something exotic, something different, captivating, practical, and surprising?

—I doubt it but I would love to sell loafers like the ones you're wearing, for instance. I've never seen leather of such a rich burgundy, I'm sure my friends would like them very much. Name a price and I'll display them in the market, it'll have to be a high price, appropriate, because in the circles I come from people don't buy by the dozen. I'll give you twenty for two dozen and arrange everything.

—That's a ridiculously low price, it doesn't even cover the cost of my trip.

—Oh please, enough cute tricks. Supply and demand. Don't forget I know what I'm talking about and while you're snoring and scratching your testicles I'm wide awake, what's more, I'm young and have no scruples. The way you walk makes me think you went to a public school where they train you to be underlings in an office. But it doesn't matter to me because you got out of all that and your situation interests me, I like your glasses and I repeat I'd like to have a picture of us together.

—I don't know, you want me to act like an Indian, some sort of native, and I'm a cosmopolitan man. . . .

—Yeah, right, today I'm starting my collection of cosmopolitan men and my career as a businesswoman. Don't forget, I'll buy the loafers from you, we'll meet in the airport, you'll hand them over to me, and I'll show them around, I have a lot of admirers and friends, I'll make them the latest rage and you'll be rich, you'll buy your own airport and won't have to walk about hiding from the police. Don't think I haven't seen you making eyes at every woman who comes along and giving bulging envelopes to the people in charge. I could turn you in to the police, show the photo I took of you with your hand in the cookie jar, and instead all I want is for us to pose for a picture together.

The picture came out fine but the frame Flora bought for it was tacky and her girlfriends made fun of her taste but behind her back because they were afraid if she got offended she'd stop providing them with those loafers that came apart so easily. Perhaps I shouldn't tell you that Walter fell hopelessly in love with Flora and quickly suffered through various phases of martyrdom: he gave her lollypops but she ridiculed him with a derisive laugh and told him more and more stories of the elixir and an exotic childhood without candy or comic books; when he brought her black transparent underclothes, she asked him if they were archeological relics so he saw they were a waste of time, no need to give him any more knowing glances; she now pointed him in the direction of the house of the chubby woman next door who'd been dying to visit them ever since they started living together in a quarter near the center; the rejections and unsuccessful presents were the only things Walter could think of before going to sleep on nights when he went to bed shivering, knowing that insomniac Flora was walking about the city or standing, hieratic, at his bedside to plan, organize, and later join the other elixir users in a session of greenish uninterrupted pandemonium.

you read me?

—Don't start in about the dance again, because I'm tired of it.
—The zoo then; you always liked that one because we were both seventeen years old and there comes the part when we were standing in front of the monkey cage and every time I fondled your ear or touched your little tit the monkey came near us and wanted to do the same, and when we started really going at it he went so crazy that the keeper came, took him out of the cage, and the four of us went to have a fuck in one of the winter pavilions and . . .
—Pig. You're mixing me up with another girl but it doesn't matter to me anymore because I've won a fortune in the lottery and I'm coming to visit you wherever you are.
—That can't be; the company would never give you my name.
—Look, don't make me laugh, because I've just come from the dentist, but no matter how far away you are from reality you must have learned that money is good for something and all those stonebroke types, poor church mice, wallflowers will wake up from their fancies of honesty when they see a wad of bills move from a wallet to their anxious sweaty hands.
—But I'm a married man.
—Hey, who's keeping the vulgar talk going. What can it possibly matter to me whether you're married, or adopted, a fakir, or whatever you please, that's not what's at stake here. . . .

One afternoon Tota cut off the call at that moment and began to take bets: fifteen that they would meet; two hundred that the littleoldlady would die of a heart attack before getting her bags packed; three that he would take a plane and come kill her. That was the week Rita began to work for the phone company; she was an old-fashioned kind of girl, and when she got angry she would pout in a sentimental, demure way. She had the voice of a fat woman; her vocal cords expanded with honied sweetness but she was so thin it would be ten years before her body evolved into the little folds and creases now lying in candy boxes, beef stews with onions and parsley, and above all the chocolate pastries that Pedro brought Monday, Wednesday, and Friday between four and five in the afternoon thanks to the generosity of the bakery on the corner that had some telephone lines illegally installed just to send bets to the branch office downtown. The Thursday that Rita joined the staff of long-distance operators Tota woke with a painful rash in her ears that meant she could only speak by opening her mouth very wide and stretching her cheeks backward to ease the itching so her hands would be free to manipulate the cables and buttons. Rita thought that Tota had smiled at her for eight hours straight and spent her first day of work planning ways to show her gratitude and loyalty over years and years to the colleague bestowed on her by good fortune and the recommendations of a friend of her uncle Fernando, who provided the high-tension cables that had been such a help in the struggle against terrorism during the first and most drastic phase of the period of national reconciliation. So Tota, without knowing how it came about and because of how cheerful she'd felt ever since playing with the skunks in the Institute, found a natural, generous, twenty-year-old ally.

—Thirty that they'll get married on their death beds

—Thixty that they'll forget the whole thing and nothing whatthoever taketh plathe.

—And this one, where'd he come from?

—Don't you know that the betting is open only to members of the long distance operators staff?

—Oh, don't thay you don't know or can't imagine how much more you could get with the help of a profethional like me; I promith you that in thome few monthz the only thing you'd have to do is path by here and collect your thalary, becauth it would rethult in looking thuthpithous if everybody left in droveth at the thame time, tho one hath to uthe a ruthe, make the callth, drink thome coffee till little by little you all thay good-bye and we thkedaddle off on vacationth.

—and how will all that be done?
—me I've always wanted to go on vacation in a cool place, in the middle of the year.
—not get broiled on a beach
—with blisters on top of that
—and spend a fortune on deodorants
—but that wouldn't be a problem because if you have money you don't need deodorant, nobody minds what rich folks smell like
—and I've seen disgusting old men with girls with figures like models
—and old women with yellow teeth and double chins with strapping young boys
—that no, now you're certainly getting into archeology, that's a thing of the past. Since they opened the Institute such things don't happen anymore. Old women, grab them, old women, shove them onto the back burner. . . .
—It's unfair, since after all we need somebody to make tasty pies, do fine embroidery, someone who keeps busy cheering when trains run on time instead of thinking the whole day of going to bed with this one or that one or of clothes, what am I going to wear or if this shirt shows the hair on my chest and then she'll want to see more. . . .
—as for me, on the other hand, I like the streets now so much more pleasant with well-dressed well-groomed people
—tho then letth do it, are you lithening to me? you underthtand me? you read me?

let's tune in

Nights they broadcast over two stations, one on TV where Rita with her fleshy lips and sweet voice took bets and the other with the respected voice of Fernando convincing radio listeners that what they were about to hear was thrilling, a slice of real life. Place your bets, dear radio listeners, place your bets. The program *Engagements of Yesteryear* needs your sentimental and prophetic contribution, place your bets, esteemed, brilliant, future romantic consultants. When the tape recording of the conversations began, the public, feeling more edgy all the time, sent in their bets by telephone, telex, special messengers, bicyclists skilled in the art of crisscrossing the city with the little book in the pocket of their jeans and in the basket a paella overloaded with saffron for those who made three consecutive bets of more than twenty thousand. The paellas were so heavy that cases of indigestion increased, pushing up the sale of antacids in a city already tense from gastritis and rapid heart beats.

—now I'm packing my bag, we'll see each other soon my love and then we'll know if we're truly sweethearts, my dear, dear boy

—let me repeat that they've paid me, I'm on salary and this is all a mistake

—as if it mattered to me how it began, what's interesting is what happens next; when I married the deceased I believed he was a ladies' man, I imagined he had a spectacular weapon inside his pants, a key to waft me away to dewy countries where he would play the cymbal, make music on my ass and later—what happened?—four children and no cymbal, and it all began in such a tremendous way, with a waltz, stolen glances, and chases; I think that you and I . . . well, something or other can happen

—but I don't think so because I'm head over heels in love

—with someone predictable for sure, same age, opposite sex . . .

Place your bets, television viewers and radio listeners. The telephones are ringing and the delicious paellas are on their way.

Place your bets and now the musical interlude begins. They played suggestive music meant to addle and muddle possibilities:
  rosita quiroga kicking wiseguys out of her pad,
  charlie and the boys of earlier times hair without brilliantine, naturally oily between the fingers of women with boy hair cuts
  lucho gatica turning out the light to think of who knows who, while tender pubescent jerk-offs were finally deciding to place their bets and be ensnarled in the love plot of the spy city crisscrossed by transmission cables so as to keep tabs on the the little-oldlady's grit versus the telephone sweetheart's resistence

Rita had become a star. Television viewers sent her perfumed letters, praised her way of dressing, assured her they liked everything about her, prepared dishes for her especially seasoned with cinnamon because she'd said she adored that color, and they wanted to watch her eat their offerings on the screen because they were a people craving instant satisfaction and Rita, let's not deny it, was now an attractive leader. She did everything Tota asked her to do and her appetite for love knew no limits, but since Tota was not at all sentimental, Rita's only contact with her came through the betting and the meals they shared after each program.
—Give me a handful of glazed almonds while we wait for the stew.
—They're good today, don't you think?
—Silly, they're like always, we live in a country with no taste, no tradition. If you only knew what I heard today. A guy called his mama from Norway to get the recipe for a birthday cake and she gave it to him with a wealth of details, and as for me, I swear, it made my mouth water because it had the most unusual ingredients that could be found only in her neighborhood and he tried to get her to give him substitutes but she didn't understand the things he mentioned in Norwegian because the products there all have different names and she was giving him brand names, then he got

very frustrated and she said send me a ticket and I'll come and make it for you, darling, for your birthday.

—And is she going?

—I think not, you know why? because he answered her in a very low voice; I'm sure she didn't hear him, because she called me back to say the call had been cut off.

—Are you sure?

—**Bitch**. I heard it clear as day because I was wearing the special earphones, the ones I use for broadcasting on cable.

beauty treatment

Teresa Jiménez bit her nails until they were left little stubs. She did it methodically. She began with the white part, going in a careful semicircle, then went on to the pink part until her teeth sank into the flesh for a brief second, enough to make an inflamed aureole. What did you do? How terrible! Impossible that you attack yourself this way, the boy's death was not your fault, it was written in the stars, it had to happen, it's fate, my dear friend, manicurist, and colleague. Don't worry about it, life has to go on, don't pull out your hair, that curl across your forehead is delicious. Something to eat, that's the ticket, something to eat, bring a few cookies or better yet a slice of chocolate cake, the caffeine will be good for you, don't cry anymore, after all the clients come here to be cheered up, don't make them feel depressed. The owner of the salon wanted her to take a vacation but she refused. Work is therapy. Work is health and you are my family above all now that I have nothing to do with my brother, the pig, look what he did to the boy, my little son, his own nephew, although they let him go free, I know he was guilty. There're things a mother senses, grasps by intuition, even though I may seem too young to be a mother, doesn't it seem odd to you that I could be, may have been, a mother considering how young I look, like a girl? Even so I have that special knowledge and I'm not going to have anything at all to do with that pervert who had the nerve to turn up at the wake after all the neighbors told me. Will you fan me a little more? Lucky that I have a nice boss and so understanding. Yes, of course, I accept your offer to take me home, I love riding in cars and maybe I'll even get some appetite back and we can stop at a restaurant with a view of the river.

Clara was walking through the city, disheveled but smiling, clothes wrinkled by her travels, when she was overcome by an irresistible desire to lie down and count her toes one by one to see if they were all still there, because Juan and Ramón had left a void she couldn't identify. She'd already touched all the orifices and had verified that nothing had been stretched and was checking the number of her teeth for the second time because she was missing two and had forgotten about the nougat that caused her to swallow them the first Christmas she spent with her in-laws, when she heard the screech of car brakes.

—What are you doing lying in the middle of the street? Don't think that you can commit suicide at my expense. Look, I already have enough problems keeping track of the accounts of the beauty salon and don't need one more. If something hurts, if you have a bruise, don't blame me, because we didn't touch you. Tell her, tell her, Teresa, because you saw the whole thing and will never testify against me.

—If she doesn't answer, the best thing would be to carry her somewhere in the car, you know? That way she could only feel grateful toward us and anyway it's starting to rain. I have the boy's bed, it's all made up and she could take a little nap. . . .

In her memory Clara had finally reached the point of those Christmases and now, relieved, was smiling, pleased by the cotillion party and the dress with polka dots her mother-in-law had given her; even though it was on the snug side, it made her feel like dancing the flamenco.

—Do you need anything? Can we take you somewhere? We want to help you to recover. Perhaps a nap, a glass of wine, a bowl of soup.

—Thank you, thank you so much. I urgently need a manicure, a haircut, a shower, the newest make-up, and a sailor's suit. Also a mask and a cigarette holder. All this is absolutely essential and if you don't provide them I'll denounce you for breach of promise

I'll curse you
turn head over heels
start a rebellion

please

dear providential strangers   help me   an untidy woman in this city will get nowhere whatsoever
    she wanders lost
visible only for the minions of the Institute
I should stand out
continue my expedition
please
off-key or not I know why I sing
you won't regret it
    pay for a beauty treatment for me   amiable generous rescuers
I'm pretty   I'm daring   I will come out with renewed pride
I'll dedicate an opera to you

—She has a nice voice, Teresa.
—Somewhat shrill and as for me songs with no danceable rhythm don't interest me.
—It's a question of taste, sometimes you have the feeling that you can't dance and the body decides otherwise. For example, the other day I was listening to some zarzuelas and a certain choreography came to me that you won't believe; this leg bent this way while the other tried to move like a figure eight and the left arm . . .
—Excellent idea. We'll go dancing together, my dear soul mates. But first, what about the treatment? Let's decide on the day, the hour, the place. We're holding up traffic and me I don't like people looking at me this way.
—Get in, get in. Don't make a scene. You never know who's listening.

Clara first took a shower in warm water and then it was into the bathtub for a soaking bath surrounded by the boy's blue ducklings. Her body had changed because of the striptease. Aside from the crotch, every inch of skin was ready for public scrutiny and that's why she told her story from the bathtub, the door open; her marriage of so many years was scattered through the details of her apprenticeship with Juan and Ramón, and Teresa, fists clenched from jealousy, smiled at her boss promising him that yes, she too would learn such things for the new addition to the beauty salon they'd been planning during the car ride.

—A magnificent idea because what's the use of a woman making herself pretty, attractive, sleek, perfumed if there's nobody to see it.

—Most of all it's an elegant idea and modern too with great commercial possibilities.

It's a ridiculous idea that will cost me a bundle and force me to attend the meetings of the cell more often. It's a son-of-a-bitching idea that messes up my ambitions, Teresa was thinking but instead of saying so she began to cry uncontrollably, with big tears and gulps and only stopped when the boss, so concerned, said to Clara: It would be better if you'd wait for us in the next room. Teresa has suffered a grave loss, her nerves are shot.

repeat after me, enunciate clearly

The instructors are nervous wrecks. They take flags of dissolved countries from the trunk, file away national anthems no longer in use, put outdated uniforms carefully wrapped in white paper in mothballs, because with the military you never know, guerrilla movements are always springing up that might make them stylish again, and they wait, poor instructors dependent on the international mail, customs, and bribes to deliver the shipment of new national symbols to them because next week will be the annual celebration of the School of Foreign Languages. Lost in thought the students wander the corridors trying out phrases of introduction and declarations of love in twenty languages since this is a modern school aware of the fact that nobody is interested in boring exercises in languages identical to themselves. Here they practice a highly migratory apprenticeship, fragmented, aimed at a new mercantile world. In the past the instructors worked as spies. For decades they served governments in exile competing for information but now they've been trained to be dependable technocrats of the fleeting word, stripped of local landscapes, stories of mommy and daddy. Their lessons are transparent, devoid of complications, an antiphilological triumph.

Roberto is the best student. He has not forgotten Clara but his enthusiasm for languages goes well beyond his original intentions and he practices constantly in a windowless cubicle with Peggy, an English tourist of Mayan origin.

—Date vuelta, turn around, je te demande because I need you inmediatamente.

—Joder, man, esto is hot, you know? Ich bin loca for you.

—Ma chérie, glaube mir, believe me, te digo la verdad, the unadulterated truth, me gusta, I like it, como los perros, doggie fashion.

Peggy hadn't felt like this since her last trip to New York. Roberto made her recall a black guy in loud tight clothes she'd coupled with laboriously in a telephone booth at five in the morning at Broadway and Forty-second street while keeping a sharp eye on her camera, which disappeared the next day anyhow while she was taking a shower at the hotel. Peggy also knows how to decipher Mayan hieroglyphics and every day after class goes back to a modest apartment where her mama has corn tortillas ready for her with stuffing minced so fine it's impossible to tell if this time she's included some of her miraculous mushrooms or not and you have to wait for several hours till the digestive process has been completed, and then the fumes rise to the brain and everything begins to boil and dance in a festival of images and sounds. Roberto is sure that his good grades will lead him to Clara's face in the city of his dreams and his sessions with Peggy will then come to an end on that bench, in the proper square at an hour convenient for them both.

The students emerge from their cubicles all at the same time. Some are sweaty, others straighten their clothes, count change, adjust ties, repair make-up, finally note down a fax number, exchange credit cards. It's been another glittering productive morning in the school. Roberto is in a hurry. He has an appointment with Rafa and will be late.

of general interest

—And you, how can my case be of interest to you? I'm innocent. That's all. The boy had lost the calcium from his bones. His mother at those meetings of the cell all the time. Who knows what they could've been planning? She always was like that, ever since she was a little girl. I remember my mom made her meals and she would eat them very nicely and then say I'm going to the store or out to the newsstand or to so-and-so's house and was gone in a flash. And only five years old, I tell you, five years old and already busy with her own affairs.
—And her mama? Why did she leave the child? Five years old, after all. Clara and I have no children, but I imagine . . .
—You imagine a lot, imagine whatever you like. The woman had her own interests. On Mondays, Wednesdays, and Fridays she went to play canasta at the house next door, on Tuesdays and Thursdays seances at home and on weekends, who knows, I wasn't around because I went to volunteer at the asylum.
—That interests me for the story. If I write that after a life of deprivations and as volunteer in the asylum what you did to the boy was a result of your traumatic childhood, people will feel sympathy for you and forgive you.
—You think so? Say that I loved the boy although he never talked to me ran and hid from me but I always found him. Behind the chair, he liked to hide there. I take it he meant to make it easier for me to grab him.

Rafa had extremely white, almost transparent, skin and since he'd been fired from the garage his nails had been clean. His job for the radio station, keeping track of the amount bet on the *Engagements of Yesteryear*, had made him really quick-fingered, also handy for his day job picking pockets on various types of public transportation.
—I'm an honest man. Right now, as you can see, I'm working as an accountant for a radio and telephone company.

—Well, that's not so interesting to people; tell me what services you performed in the asylum.
—Services, no, services as such, no. I went there voluntarily as an orphan. On weekends some families would take children from the asylum for outings. I knew some of them from the park, and when they were taken out they had to leave behind the gray overalls worn as uniform at that time. It was a different time, you know, everybody wore an identifying uniform so there could be no mistaking the person you were dealing with. But today it's a mess, because the clothing manufacturers prefer us all to go about as impostors, you realize how nice it would be if we all wore uniforms? Anyway they left me a pair of overalls that I put on. On weekends young priests from another parish came to minister to the asylum. I was one of their favorites. To Rafa they gave everything; Rafa, they said, is a model orphan, because I was very docile and those cute little clerics with that naughty and saintly air I always found delicious.
—And they never realized you were an impostor?
—How do I know? The one who turned me in did so for another reason. Years later when my beard started to sprout they said I wasn't a boy anymore, couldn't receive any more benefits, and this, that, and the other. The overalls had been too small for me for some time. I personally think it was out of jealousy or spite because I didn't want to go to the seminary.
—Your sister says you were always a pervert and is convinced the boy wouldn't have died if you hadn't abused him. Bloodsucker. That's the word she used.
—Do you want to write this story to exonerate me or to repeat the garbage you read in women's magazines?
—Rafa, I have my own reasons. I'm searching for my wife. I want her to see my name in the newspapers. Well-known journalist. I want her to realize I'm a famous man, original, unbiased, polyglot, and to regret having left me. I'm going to write something unheard

of about your case but I need more material. As of now there's nothing sensational enough to give me the name and recognition I'm looking for.

—You're insulting me.

—Oh stop your accusations. Enough, I'm tired and I'm going to Peggy's house to eat tortillas.

—I tell you your article has to say the obvious, the truth that demonstrates once and for all that this civilization is based on little white lies. Put **Mother guilty of boy's death** and you'll see how famous you'll become.

Marisita walks as if she had bells in her shoes. She sways. They saw her take off her suit jacket and sneeze so hard the buttons popped off her washable raw-silk blouse they brought her from Hong Kong. The nameless women are standing in line, waiting to be given a name, a number, a file, and to be added to the list. Josefina looks at them and lets out shrieks of pleasure. Enthusiasm drives her. She wants to bring sanity into the Institute. She wants to prove these women are not truly ugly. She wants them to be returned to the street. She wants to take their fingerprints. Nude photos. Dress them as apaches. Have them pose in black negligees. Marisita has a mission and is all gung-ho

   feverish
   efficient
   with elixir sneezes
   leaning on Josefina
   seated at the table
   watcher from the terrace

marisita has become a sleepless heroine. Her only payment consists of the songs of Josefina, who is now making acrobatic whirls, laughing and calling to the crowd

     come
        come
           big
               girls

no tickets needed it's free   marisita our legal adviser our dear lawyer who watches over us   come come and give your information to marisita format   my favorite lawyer   my frenetic superelegant career woman.

Marisita couldn't pause a second, she didn't hear the protests of the ones who'd given up and she wasn't bothered by hints of suicide. The numerous signs of apathy that proliferated in the dim wards of the Institute meant nothing to her. She'd spent so much money on manicures and waxings that she didn't see the women,

pale, with rheumy skin, unmoisturized cheeks. She walked past them as if they were part of the walls. That's why she said in a serious tone to the deputy director while arranging forms in her briefcase: You have to do something about the Institute. Repaint it or put up some posters of rock stars, the atmosphere is so oppressive here. If you like, I'll make the request to the ministry myself, they're expecting me tonight in any case. We've approved a new budget
    dotted the i's
        reevaluated all our legal programs
            congratulated ourselves   approved trips   perks
and tonight we'll party with lots of laughs I can't invite you because you're invisible, an employee of a secret company, but I will help you because I recognize your importance to my career and I find you likeable despite the smell of sweat from your rubber boots.
—What a pleasure to have met an understanding woman at last, a woman who wants to do something for me, give me something. Can you grant me a few brief instants? I want to confess something to you.
—Why not? But I have to leave very soon, as you know.
—For several nights now I've thought of you. When you leave the Institute I feel it becomes empty all of a sudden. I don't feel like talking to anyone. Mornings the hope that you might come to do your volunteer work inspires me, makes me take a shower, put on cologne . . .
—Almost the same as when I started to take the elixir.
—I don't sleep and I only eat if I imagine we're doing it together.
—Let's go out to a restaurant. We'll charge it to the ministry. Thank you for the information. I have to go. They're expecting me.
—Marisita, Dr. Format, you don't understand. I'm desperately in love with you, I can't live without you, let's eat together, make love, fill out forms together. Anything at all. Together.

—They'd told me there were still such people. Interesting. We'll talk more about it some other day.
—Tomorrow. I invite you to go dancing tomorrow.
—Don't be funny. I don't have time for such things. Why not invite Josefina de la Puente? She loves to dance. I think she was doing a *paso doble* today or maybe it was a *jota*; in any case something Spanish and lively.

it's the kind of thing that goes to a woman's head

—The face looks very nice.
—A bit sickly.
—Better that way. Men like women a little pale. It makes them think the women have spent a lot of time lying between the sheets and they could crawl in bed with them, give them kisses, and squeeze them until they'd get some color in their cheeks for the very first time. Then they'd pull the covers up very gently . . .
—Go out with them on a rainy night and lend them a raincoat that's too big
—underneath she's naked, the pale woman, and only stops trembling when he caresses her with his rough hands beneath the raincoat.
—Her skin is soft because she uses our products
—and then they'll never ever forget that night
—every time it rains he'll have an erection and the police will say it's inexplicable, that nobody can say why a decent man would go out to rape foreign women, because the rape victims are always foreign. . . .
—They don't notice the rapes occur only when it rains
—they never notice such things, the only thing that interests them is to take the statements from the women and pump them for details to repeat when they get home to thrill their wives and make up for the boredom of waiting up for their husbands and not knowing what they're involved in during the day
—In any case we'll have to put some rouge on her cheeks, people shy away from thin pale faces. They think they have the sickness and avoid them. Thin and pale, yes, if you want to arouse old men. Personally I believe a brownish rouge would suit her better, gives a hint of the sea.
—It goes perfectly with the sailor suit, I love it. But the lips for sure have to be red. Crimson.
—Hurry, this is a paying establishment and we can't spend so much time on charity cases. Look at the line. The women waiting

in the street are getting desperate. If a van from the Institute passes by and sees them standing there looking like that, who knows what might happen.

—And the tooth. I want you to paint a landscape on this tooth. A waterfall. Flowers and a nightingale. Afterwards cover it with enamel and it'll stay put.

Teresa was no longer bothered by jealousy. She'd realized Clara had other plans in mind and while she made a complicated miniature landscape appear on one of her teeth she was gradually captivated by the destiny that Clara had chosen for herself. She felt the coolness of the waterfall on her heels and heard the nightingale's song, sharp and pure, cutting through the fumes of the acetone, the lotions for permanents, the depilatory creams and rinses. Suspended between her existence and the promise of Clara's voyage, she longed to be Clara's friend, to go with her.

—Shall we go together? I can help you, touch up the tooth if need be. Make sure your make-up doesn't run.

—I don't know. I'm very absent-minded. I'll forget you're with me.

—Please. You decide everything and I'll follow.

—But I understand your nerves are shot. Your boss, who's treated me so well, told me so.

—Actually it's not so bad. I have some savings and I really want to go, let me go with you and you can see how it works out. I'll arrange my affairs with the cell and be ready early in the morning.

—The cell?

—It takes a long time to explain but is not so difficult to understand. All women should assume certain political obligations, observe certain standards of general behavior. We prepare ourselves in the cell, we train ourselves for when things change. I must tell my companions so they won't feel abandoned and so they can find a substitute for me on Thursdays when it's my turn to take notes of the meeting and collect the fees.

—My dear, I have no idea what you're talking about. I'm a little sailor in search of adventure.

—See, that's exactly what I need to learn. The way you just moved your cigarette holder and arched your left eyebrow. And that tooth. What a great idea. It didn't strike me at first but now that I look at it closely . . .

—Oh come on, just go to your cell. I'll wait for you at your house. I'll take a rest in the boy's bed.

Instead of going to the cell, Teresa made the first mistake of her voyage and went to the bank to withdraw the money she'd collected as treasurer, added it to what she'd stolen an hour earlier from the cash register of the beauty salon, and with a sigh of satisfaction carefully hid it among the curls of the permanent she'd got the week before. I didn't even know I was going to need them, she said to herself, congratulating herself on the curls. At that moment Teresa was happy. She was a woman who loved keeping secrets and the hoard of bills in her hair made her feel like a queen. Finally she felt the gravity of her body, what the bills can do, the bills I managed to get, those I've swindled, all for our trip. Oh, Teresa was so pleased. She didn't know that Rafa's statement would appear the next day in all the newspapers of the entire country and would be telexed to households in various parts of the planet where self-sacrificing mothers would embrace their children while asking themselves where such a monster had come from and the answer, **from a beauty salon,** would overwhelm entire peoples who'd have to modify their erotic fantasies, thus posing a threat to an economy based on the production of cosmetics. But it's too early for all this because Teresa and Clara are just preparing for their meeting and no intuition gave them any warning they'd be pursued by Interpol and all the local police forces, to say nothing of the ferocious minions of the cell. No intuition alerted them to the danger even though they were women. Within the hour they'll be eating pizza together and together will polish the tooth while Teresa attends to the elaborate, rich, and surreptitious fortune.

she acts up

Something has terrified Josefina de la Puente. She hadn't wanted to appear for her morning meeting with Marisita. Of her own accord she's shut up in a cell with flowered paper on the walls, and she's counting. She begins with the petals, then the stems, and in a trance proceeds to the hairs on her arms. It's an easy task but possible only by concentrating to the utmost. She can't eat, go to the bathroom, brush her teeth. The enumeration is inexorable, each higher number creates its own sounds, its particular landscape. The cell grows huge and then Josefina starts singing jungle hymns because she's traveling through vast wonders of the Amazon, crossing rivers nestled between mountains, has to kill poisonous snakes determined to get at her legs. Josefina toils on exhausted but persists throughout days and nights until she hears the voice of an Andalusian woman who was kidnapped by Indians in 1842; Josefina is enraptured by the woman's language, a mixture of Spanish, Portuguese, and Guaraní. Speaking in a strange felicitous fashion, she asks Josefina not to rescue her because she prefers to stay kidnapped. But that, yes, she's very much in need of a visit, someone to come and keep her company because the new century has brought in surly mine workers and done away with the Indians of earlier times. She's preserved her youth in that humid climate filled with nutritious natural products but nobody is aware of it since each generation thinks she's a tourist who speaks with the birds. Definitely, she needs company. Josefina says she's ready, should leave. They should let her out, buy her a ticket. Serve her a *feijoada*. She's ravenously hungry. No. Don't interrupt me. I must listen to what Filomena is saying to me, my luscious Andalusian. Go away, I don't need you. Leave me with my dear friend.

therapy

—I'm really tired, Camila. Let's stop for a while. Give me some coffee even if it's cold.
—I don't care if you are tired, let's keep going. I'm paying you by the hour.
—Well, all right, but then I won't do the gypsy dance. Something slower, a more restful rhythm.
—But that doesn't do a thing for me.
—Ah, no. You don't realize it because it requires more concentration. I've discovered that when I'm not upset a more subtle music comes to my body and then, if you look at me, it's really marvelous because each one of my pores oozes a great calm and I feel that all together they say to me: Make an arch with your arms, a trampoline leap with the legs, slowly. The floor is foam rubber. Look at me, look at me carefully and now concentrate on my big toe. See how it arches upward, the nail grows soft and thinks of its own affairs. First the left, then the right. No, no. Don't let your mind wander. You shouldn't take off your stockings. Simply think and try to get into this dance.
    it's not like the others
       without a partner
         it's for thinking
little by little you too will feel the calm. No. Don't blink your eyes. If they feel tired, close them and sink into the dance because it's a mattress
    so comfortable no pillow is needed   I'll take care of you camila come lie down   don't worry about anything   keep quiet very quiet

What a relief for Rogelio when Camila, exhausted, fell asleep on the living-room sofa. The house was large and dark with heavy brocade curtains revealing snowy landscapes in ochre and reddish colors, every once in a while a little girl waved toward a dog lost among the folds. A thick layer of dust covered the piano. Photographs of newly wed couples in old-fashioned clothes decorated the surfaces of the mahogany furniture. A tennis player with very white teeth held up his racket in one of the pictures while a girl with braces on her teeth looked straight at the camera as she tried to pat a recalcitrant German shepherd. That afternoon while Camila was sleeping, Rogelio recognized her. She was dreaming of the tennis club and suddenly grimaced, making her face the same as the one in the photograph. Don't think Rogelio was at all moved by that. Camila had turned him into an ordinary hired hand. He immediately took note of the tennis club, the racket, and planned his next dance. It cost him more and more effort to earn his salary from Camila. He had lost the knack of the beginning when his every movement sparked recognition in Camila, a sigh, congratulations. For some time the hours spent with her consisted of disagreeable discussions of financial matters with her blaming him for being dense and him, lost in memories of Josefina, replying distractedly that he was doing his best, and **of course** as sure as money in the bank she would come out of the treatment with an inner life. Camila wanted to have friends, someone to go to the zoo with, to bring a good-looking guy with sweaty hands home with her some afternoon around a quarter to six so that later they could go out to eat after showering with hair still damp, and they'd gaze at each other during the antipasto the way she'd seen so many couples do in restaurants. For all that she needed an inner life. It was inevitable. She would have to confess things of the past: I tell you because I trust you after all we've lived through together, I don't know how to put it into words, you're the only one, there's something about our relationship that makes it possible for me to say so many things I never dreamed I would tell but now I've changed. Camila arranged her hair so as to suggest an interesting past filled with stories, minuets, ambiguous touches; Rogelio was her vehicle for getting something that others possessed without making any apparent effort.

Rogelio stretched out like a lizard on another sofa placed exactly parallel to Camila's so he could watch the rhythmical movements of her mass of golden curls out of the corner of his eye. Before calculating the fee for this session he measured once more the amount that separated him from Josefina. It was enormous. Now it was unbearable for him to live without following the woman of the doorknob; his exile from the streets through which he pursued her was made possible by his love with Josefina and brought on uneasy feelings much like insomnia and failure.

—I don't want you to put me to sleep again. This little trick of a nap and hypnosis smells like quackery to me. I want us to talk, I want you to teach me or make me remember or whatever because this summer I have to go to the beach on vacation with a terrific sweetheart. I've picked out a great bikini I'll show you after a while. But we have to concentrate on my facial expression . . . suggestive, I want it to be suggestive. Otherwise nobody will be interested in me.
—I believe that sleep does a lot of good. Lying beside you that way I channel my impressions and thoughts to you and you absorb them passively.
—Charlatan. You know very well that what I'm after are your dances and not your naps.
—In that case, I don't see why I have to spend my afternoons here, I'll go back to the circus, rehearse, that life suits me better, and you'll save the two hours of rest. . . .
—No, no. Come on, Rogelio, don't be offended. You know very well I enjoy eating cookies after the nap. Don't stop coming. I've still got some money. We've got enough for several years of sessions.
—Well, just so it's clear. I'm not the one who's insisting. I'm leaving now, it's getting late, I have an appointment.
—Yesterday, too.

—I'll try to come earlier tomorrow. . . .

—And the cookies?

Now you know. At that moment Camila's expression was like the one of the girl with the braces. Rogelio left whistling a song whose origin he didn't recognize. It has an Andalusian air, he said to himself before buttoning his jacket, because the way the southeast wind was blowing he was likely to get chilled to the bone.

wouldn't it be something to have a windproof umbrella

First some big black swollen drops began to fall, sweeping away the filth and soot from the factories, then came an intermittent rain with sunny breaks during which people went to meetings, bought toilet paper and beans in the markets, and sat in cafés to eat sandwiches gone moldy from the humidity until time to get up and go. Day after day. A sky the color of lead and the wind fiercer all the time went howling through buildings with broken windows. The thunderclaps were giant belches, followed by a grotesque hail that gouged holes in the pavement as well as in the poor-quality metal of the automobiles imported by the under secretary of transportation as part of a deal that would be uncovered ten years later.

 Rita was waiting for her shift in the station when she realized she couldn't get back home. She was surrounded by baskets of goodies sent by television viewers roused by her fleshy lips. She ate the treats delicately on the screen. Live and direct, ladies and gentlemen, Rita takes pleasure in working for you live and direct. As the months went by Rita gained weight, filled with the affection of a public that also made bets on her figure: That little roll of fat belongs to me, they said proudly in their homes when she appeared on the television screen. No. It's mine. Don't you see it's shaped like the chocolate pudding with almond paste? It takes longer for pies to be metabolized; you can see it beneath that transparent dress. How gorgeous she is! Nothing like she was when she began. The telephone company and TV station were a cozy home for Rita, who, so happy, anticipated what the public and her colleagues wanted. They all loved her but very few sensed the secret of her dedication, the key of that enthusiasm meant to delight, the reason for the loyalty with which she buttered them up. She was a virgin. She was waiting. With each chocolate she made herself illusions of eternal love. Such a situation filled her with tenderness for her own self. That's why all of you will understand why when she got out of bed in the morning she washed her right hand with a special soap and began to use one glove, of a scandalous red. When they asked her why, she would say coyly: My fiancé . . .

The lights at the station were off. The storm intensified. There was a certain amount of confusion at first but soon, by feel, they all settled themselves in corners that were more or less dry. Except Rita. She wasn't familiar with the nooks and crannies of the ancient building that seventy years back had been used as home for wounded acrobats, gladiators mutilated by lions, *écuyères* with spines shattered during the golden age of wild circuses. Rita's one and only instinct was the one that kept her close to her public. With her back against a rough wall she strained for the sound of a breath, a sigh that would orient her, but the metallic sound of the hail as it hit the nearby rooftops, most likely tin, interfered.

—Come, give me your hand, I'll take you to a safe spot.

—I can't see a thing. Where are you?

—Do you feel my boot between your legs? Come, don't be afraid; don't huddle against that wall, you'll catch cold; it always gets cold when it rains.

—Everything's so dark. Where are the others?

—Rita, Rita, close your pretty mouth. Or better yet, kneel down and open it, I have a surprise for you.

Obedient, greedy, she licked, sucked a long time until, covered with semen, she fell in a puddle and he lifted her in his arms because working as a cameraman had developed his muscles and it was no effort to carry her through the labyrinths of the station to the acrobats' rehabilitation room, which had been closed off since the function of the building had changed. He laid her on a stretcher and began to tickle her with a feather, running it over her and penetrating her with it better than Rita herself had been able to do with her right hand. At this point Rita's eyes had adjusted to the darkness and she saw Heriberto undressing with care because he'd been poor as a kid and didn't want to ruin his clothes. However, she didn't want to let on that she knew what was happening. Ashamed, she tore off her clothes in a rush. Suddenly, legs opened, she wanted to let it happen. But Heriberto gave her a smack and said:

—Don't be so easy, girl. I'll give it to you but I have my fancies. I'll let you have it but

    you have to woo me

        you have to convince me

           dance

           use the trampoline

      show me the treasures you keep so well hidden

Hours. Days. Ferocious, humid training. She learned. Heriberto was not so dumb. He had a business deal in mind. Plans for after the rain. He had to soften up the territory. So that Rita, red-hot, would sign a contract:

—My star, my slut, my treasure.

—But I'm already the star of *Engagements of Yesteryear*.

—That's nothing. I mean international star.

—But I can't do anything without instructions.

—Sexy movies, dear heart. With your talent, your curves, we'll set the movie houses of the world on fire. Amsterdam, New York, Tandil, Villa Luro.

—I'll be so embarrassed when people recognize me. I hardly know what to do.

—I'll guide you as always, my dearest one. I'll tell you everything you have to do from the tiniest little fart up to the place and exact moment of the contortions. When, how, and why. With whom and how much we charge.

—Heriberto, I'm dying to fuck. With your hand at least, don't be so mean.

—No. No. First to plan our future, my darling. We'll get married the minute the rain stops.

—My love.

—I always wanted to marry a virgin.

—I'll give you my red glove. I don't need it anymore.
—Here's the boot
of our first touch.
—(*Both together*) For the museum of our love. For all the countless anniversaries of this story.

My dears:

The happiness of this pair is complete at this moment. They adore one another with no suspicions. When Rita discovers that Heriberto installed a special camera that recorded her deflowering and apprenticeship, she'll pretend to be indignant. With pouts and clicking her tongue she'll scold and threaten him, but when he goes out to look for a leading man with enormous genitals to be her movie partner she'll go search for the tape and open-mouthed, admiring, will watch it over and over again.

in the country

Poor poor things, the rain had caught them right in the middle of their trip. Clara's sailor suit is a mass of wrinkles. Teresa had to rescue the bills she was keeping in her curls and stash them in her underclothes. They are walking along a slippery path bordered by trees and clusters of forget-me-nots. It's no use hoping the weather will get better any time soon, it's been raining for two days now with no letup. Teresa has not shown Clara the money; she keeps at a distance, protective hand over her stomach to keep the bills from being ruined. Until they saw the hotel.

—Teresa, Teresa. Have you ever seen such a modern castle? With so many floors and windows? And those red bushes at the entrance! Wait, I think I see a porter in uniform behind the glass door. What a surprise for a little sailor like me! Oh, if we only had the money to go in, get our clothes dried, have a shelter from this terrible weather. . . .

—Let's try to get in, they may even take pity on us and let us stay for nothing.

—Never, never. If I dressed myself as a sailor it's to show my independence. Better to stay like this outside, the sun will come out and dry my clothes and I can go on with my plans. You do whatever you like. If you want to be a beggar, or turn prostitute, or become a cook in some stranger's house . . .

—Enough speeches, not for nothing did I leave the cell. If I'd known you'd also turn out to be into politics, I would've stayed where I was because actually I had quite a good future in the beauty institute, with women so eager to follow my advice and my boss ready to be caught. Who knows how far . . .

—how far
  how far
    and what for?
      Teri Teri
  what do you want?
a mask so merry

  a disguise
 nothing else otherwise
   with a disguise
 up down and sidewise

—I'm not going to discuss it. It has rhythm, it's true, and to thank you I have a surprise. I can pay. I invite you to the castle that is a hotel, don't be naive. Let's get there before nightfall because their lights must have been cut off like everywhere else in the city.

—What luck to be in such well-heeled company!

—But do me a favor and talk normally because people don't like to have their lives complicated by incomprehensible little games.

—Again you insult me. This is not a little game even if it seems incomprehensible to you. You should get something straight since you're following me like an unfurled shadow. Admit you're curious and I'll agree. Admit you're enjoying our trip.

—We'll talk about it later. Let me inquire by myself, you hide behind that tree and when they say yes, I'll call you. I don't think they'll be taken in by the sailor suit.

  Teresa wanted to arrange everything quickly so she wouldn't have to spend her loot. She was so right, only later would she know how right, as events kept revealing to her the pattern of the happenstances of her life. When the porter saw her he recognized the drenched duckling of the bedtime story his mama had read to him every night until he was eighteen years old. His eyes grew moist with emotion; he had looked for that expression in a face for fifty-five years and this storm had brought it to him in the form of a woman stiff with cold and with her hands clasped over her stomach.

—Certainly you may come in. You and your companion. You said she was a disguised girlfriend? Well, I don't wish to be indiscreet but I would like to ask you a personal question.

—If you are wondering why I'm holding my hands over my stomach, it's the cold. Once I have my private bath and dry clothes, I'll be back to normal. You'll see. It's nothing bad or contagious, nothing special, alarming, or mysterious.

—No, No. Excuse my boldness, but I wished to know, well, your civil status. Are you married?

As always before answering, Teresa made a calculation and this time decided to tell the truth. In a tremulous voice she told him her unfortunate story, her early widowhood, the death of the boy but left out the details of her relationship with her boss, the cell, the theft.

—Come in, Armando Casona at your service. And your friend? Let's not forget about her.

They had to carry Clara in, curled in a ball, shivering from the rain, huddled in the sailor suit, which had not withstood the siege of the weather and was in tatters. Armando couldn't contain his emotion. He wanted to show off his power to Teresa, mobilize all the luxuries of his hotel just for her. He decided to assign them adjoining rooms with a view of the swimming pool and promised that as soon as the rain stopped he would have exotic delicacies served to them to the accompaniment of harp concertos. In the meantime, they'd have to make do with candlelight and the dark blue blankets he had brought up from the basement since the hotel was intended for summer vacationers who came to relax during the hottest months. A dozen guerrilla fighters grown wealthy from the sudden hike in the price of weapons occupied the lower floor; Teresa went to sleep lulled by revolutionary slogans in different languages. Clara didn't even realize where she was until the following morning because she fell asleep the minute they laid her on the mattress that had been perfumed with sedatives by the pedophile who'd spent three nights there the week before. As usual Armando walked through the corridors all night long, making sure everything was in order, but this time he was humming snatches of boleros he'd heard on the radio during the broadcasts of *Engagements of Yesteryear*. He was one of the loyal and constant bettors and now was promising himself a telephone romance with Teresa. We'll be famous. We'll be eternal. People will place bets on our destiny. At last. Like the littleoldlady. I'll have to leave the country. We'll talk day and night. Everybody will think of us. They'll spend their savings, send us letters, lubricate their siestas with our love.

Armando was making plans impatiently because he was somewhat bothered by the idea that at his age the legend of his romantic abilities should not be better known. At around three in the morning, when the guerrillas, coming off their drunken spree, stopped making an uproar, he chose his alias. Latin Lover.

these loafers pinch my toes

Walter's approach to the manufacture and sale of loafers was to use the personal touch. First: go to the plant, convince the foreman it would be to his benefit to sell him each day's overrun for a ridiculous price that would still make him a millionaire in a few years. Second: increase the productivity of the workers by slipping a few drops of the elixir into their midday coffee. Third: intercept delivery trucks until a driver can be found who'd agree to transport cargo in exchange for shares of stock in a touristic complex under construction in a remote, idyllic region of the Amazon. The system worked very well because there were numerous loafer factories in the city and Walter created competition based on invented rumors of fabulous earnings, worrisome for the plants he had not yet contacted.

Flora listened to what Walter was saying without any interest but felt she had to pretend she was paying attention and, with a grin à la Claudette Colbert, asked for details while counting out the bills she should pay him. Walter was very confused. He wasn't used to being paid by a ten-year-old girl and his pride conspired against his own interests.

—Well, count it, is that right? Look, I don't want you coming to me with the tune that I'm dishonest and you want to go smuggle your stuff through the airport again.

—No, it's fine, fine. I believe you, don't worry. So your little girlfriends like the loafers? Do they wear them with pleated skirts? A man of my age doesn't pay attention to the styles of young people. When I was a student loafers went very well with a blue blazer. . . .

—They wear them with anything at all, we don't have the patience to wear pleated skirts. My commercial venture is successful because I don't get involved with the whole business of what goes with what. Walter, sometimes your naiveté amazes me. It must be because you slept all that time. Eight, nine hours and on top of that a nap? I don't understand how; if the elixir could be sold freely, I'd give you a little just so you could see the difference, although at your age I don't know if it would have any effect.

—I like to sleep, you should try it sometimes. It's easy. You go to bed and sometimes you dream.

—In one way or another you have to compensate for the lack of activity in your life. I adore nighttime and speaking of that, it's getting dark and the rain has put me way way behind. Today all my clients must be waiting for me. It's the first more or less dry day in almost a month.

—Shall I go with you? I'm not tired. It must be the change in the weather. I feel rejuvenated, I'd love to see your little friends, help you with the sales. . . .

—If you do, it'll be for free. I'm not interested in sharing the earnings and you'll have to come with me to load the boxes. That takes the most time.

—Believe me when I tell you the only reason I'm doing this is simply to find out for myself what the consumer public is like, to get a firsthand look at the reality of the demand.

—Why not just say you're curious? Or that you'd like to see how you can grab my part of the business? Don't think you're going to fool me just like that. You sign this admission of guilt for crimes against the boy. If you betray me in the business, I'll turn it over to the police.

—Crimes against the boy? What are you talking about? The whole world knows the uncle was guilty, and in any case it hasn't been proved that the death was due to criminal acts.

—Yeah, say whatever you please, but if the police find a guilty party who has signed a confession and the testimony of a friend of the boy who swears she saw them going together into a hotel with rooms to rent by the hour . . . On top of that, you're not married and with those tight clothes you don't have to look very far to . . .

—What a fantasy you've come up with. No wonder you don't need to dream, with that calculating little brain and such an inventive imagination. . . . So you were a friend of the boy? I thought he was rather poor, from another neighborhood, not like you and your crowd. He wasn't an elixir kid.

—You would think of that but don't forget that nobody really knows what the boy's life was like because nobody paid any attention to him. I can say whatever I please. That we drank milk together during the summer in the national camp for mathematically gifted children, or we rehearsed together in the choir, or I knew him when we were both volunteers in the city clean-up campaign when those caramel candies in the sticky wrappers were all the rage, or we played together in the park when he escaped from the neighborhood because he was afraid of the uncle, although at bottom that was a false accusation because Rafa is innocent and I can testify to it. I have the confession of the real guilty one. A stranger. Children should not talk to strangers. Everybody knows that. As you see, you have to sign.

—I'll sign it if you like because I know I'm not going to be betrayed by some little girl no matter how many times I sign, and, Flora, don't forget to give the document back to me the minute we get back from our walk.

—That no. If you sign, I'll keep the document as long as our association lasts.

—And if I don't sign?

—If you don't, sleep well, Walter. I don't need it. The idea was yours. And now hurry because I have to go. . . .

—You have the document all prepared? What intuition. Good. There you are. Shall we go in my car?

Flora gives him precise instructions. It's already night when they arrive at a brightly lit business district where images of Donald Duck and Mickey Mouse alternate with booths showing instruments of electronic communication, video games, and very high slides that come down into restaurants offering Chinese, Mexican, and Japanese food. All fast, very fast, so people won't spend much time eating. What an intelligent generation, Walter would have said aloud if Flora had been at his side, but she'd gone to chat, distribute boxes of loafers all but snatched out of her hands by little girls with angelic faces and alert expressions. There is also a baby crawling around alone until a teenage nanny remembers it, grabs it up with a joyful shout, gives it a cookie, and dances a quick dance with it before depositing it in a space surrounded by a red fence where other smiling babies are playing with rubber balls and asymmetric blocks. Flora's coming has set off a to-and-fro in the streets, and Walter sees girls and boys climb down from lighted balconies, emerge from side streets, and surround her. Standing on a garbage can, light, precise, she says to them:

> No boys here
>   we don't need them
>   these loafers are for girls
>   excellent quality   stylish colors   unusual prices
>   better than seven-league boots
>   loafers
>   better than a magic carpet
>   no returns
>   because they're perfect
>   will give you just what you're looking for
>   with the ideal support
>   flying comfortable
>   loafers from feet to head

At that moment the girls began chanting FEET TO HEAD! FEET TO HEAD! and clever practical Flora went about collecting money and distributing the remaining boxes. The boys drifted off, slowly at first, like chased dogs, but they were young and soon in threes and fours they'd come up with some sort of entertainment inside the houses with the lighted balconies. Even though he hadn't slept at all that night, Walter was kept awake by the surprising discovery of this area of the city and he wasn't mistaken when he saw one of the girls put on a pair of loafers that was too small and a greenish liquid start seeping through the stitching.

hear the little birds sing

Marisita spread-eagled. Marisita snores, twists, shouts, turns over, disturbed, opens her eyes with a fixed, catatonic look, and collapses into a chair. That's how she'd been for months in the Institute. During the rainy period she couldn't get back to her apartment to pluck her eyebrows to give them that authoritarian arch that set her apart, couldn't eat the strawberries Elena had given her for helping with the registration of her daughter as a newborn despite the evidence to the contrary and the words she'd spoken in the delivery room. The row of minuscule green vials of the elixir in the bathroom medicine cabinet, trophy of her salary, passport to wakefulness, remained intact for seven and a half weeks until Rafa, now working full time as a hustler, was tipped off by the porter and opened the door with a credit card. He took all the vials except one because he saw Marisita's picture on a table in the living room and found her appealing. Without the elixir her body suffered a short circuit and Dr. Marisa Format was turned into a succession of convulsions, hiccups, vomiting. Josefina, stunned, saw how the color of her eyes changed, noticed the grimace of her mouth but felt no pity for her until, during one of the many nights when she was applying cold compresses to her forehead, she seemed to recognize in the moans the voice of Filomena, the luscious Andalusian. So she began to tell Filomena stories of her life, to give her all the facts that would let her shed the gelatinous part of her existence.

—Filomena, I'm so happy you've finally come to visit me. Getting to the Amazon would be hard for me because they keep me shut up in this building, why, I'm not sure. In any case, it doesn't bother me because we're together; the other women are somewhat boring, I shouldn't criticize them because in general they're good companions; they just seem shallow to me, the opposite of you, Filomena, a woman who comes from far away, from another era, with a past and not a frustrated housewife, a widow of one single husband, a schoolgirl looking for a sweetheart or a lesbian in love with the gym teacher. From the start I liked the idea of being closed in; I like hearing voices, transmitting them, and with Rogelio, my husband, I had to talk always in the same tone or pretend to be dreaming aloud because I could see all that made a big impression on him. My states of mind. He called them my states of mind. He wanted to be married to a woman who was the same day after day. Imagine, Filomena, I ended up with an absolutely monogamous husband and then he didn't want to know anything about the visits I had day after day. In bed, without my saying a word to him, he was bothered by my changes of speed, of voice. He went after me between the sheets, begged me to reject him, and when he reached me—because, of course, the good thing was we enjoyed the business and there, yes, we got along very well—he would mutter something about a dooknob. In code. He muttered in code and imagine that after so many years of marriage I didn't know what the whole thing of the doorknob was, but he begged me, pleaded, ordered me to be silent.

   don't talk to me, precious
      there, right there, that's good
         I found you
           but say nothing to me
   you don't know me
   don't change   don't call me rogelio   don't call yourself josefina
      quietquiet
      a little more there
   that's how I like it

and on and on he talked to me, fondled me, and from then on I went in tune with the voices of my grandmother and my mama. Words rose up from my innards and I wanted to sing, to show him we were a group, closer than the girl scouts, ties of blood, a serious affair. But by then he was already snoring. He's not a bad guy, Rogelio. A bit dull, with his feet on the ground or in a place where I never go.

The thing is we got to know each other when we were very young. Rogelio was in a business that paid quite well. He worked in a dance school. Couples came to learn how to dance for wedding celebrations, engagement parties, or the boys showed up so they could go to dances and impress the girls, *Come I'll show you*, look, I heard them and they were interested in only one of two things: to pick up the girl or dance like an awkward clown, paying no attention to the partner, so when they asked me to dance I already knew I wouldn't see good steps or anything, I was never interested in getting the boys to pay attention to me; Filomena, don't jump around that way, let's see, close your eyes, the bulging look doesn't suit you. I'll serve your little eyes back to you on a tray if you misbehave. It's a shame the greenish color you used to have is fading, it reminded me of the jungle. When you're better you'll tell me about it. Lucky that you're no longer throwing up. I think you scared off the director and the deputy director for good, they get into a sweat up to their eyeballs in those rubber suits they wear every time they come to see us. They're afraid of the sickness. Poor, stupid, empty-headed things, they don't realize it's simply a phenomenon of adaptation. Such a long trip. From the tropics. What do they want. I explained it to them, I acted it out, but they didn't even pay attention.

let them stay together
have their meals sent in
let the de la Puente woman take care of her

I heard them dictating the report. We are safe from those fools, Filomena. So I signed up for the dance classes because I wanted to have fun with no strings attached. I began going every day at two in the afternoon. Rogelio wore tight blue pants that let every movement he made be seen, muscle by muscle. I found his legs enchanting and when we danced I grazed them on purpose so all that knowledge would permeate my hands and the rest of the body. The owner of the ballroom didn't like it. One day, vulgar as she was, she came in saying I was a pig and Rogelio, to make matters worse, had a milky spot on his fly; she told him to put me out into the street to make sure I would never come back again. That's how we got started, Filomena. A very good way, don't you think? Between classes I would wait for him behind the building in an alley, and hidden by delivery wagons and garbage cans, we danced until I got him under my skin. Filomena, laugh a little, I just made a joke. Don't worry, next time. Look, you've been sleeping for weeks. I hadn't realized that the time change was such a serious thing. Obviously, since I've never been anywhere.

fame and fortune

The littleoldlady arrives at the airport ready to meet the sweetheart of yesteryear, prepared to spend a bundle on private detectives, telephone-sniffing dogs, bribes to unscrupulous telephone operators who will say no problem, no old dodo needs money, but she doesn't know that the porter carrying her bags has a secret that would be of more interest to her. That's why he strides with almost military step through the corridors of the airport and runs straight into Walter, who, since Flora no longer comes to his house, spends his time searching for her all over and, failing to find her, mutters a constant stream of scathing recriminations against her; the littleoldlady is keeping her sentimentality for the ideal sweetheart. Wallet bulging with bills, her shoes suddenly feel too tight, and one of the pearl buttons of her blouse pops off when she tries to take a deep breath. The porter will not realize she's lying in a faint on the floor with a thread of blood coming from her mouth until he hears Walter's scream. It's no use trying to help her in order to get a good tip. The airport EMTs come with a stretcher. Three nurses with identical blond pony tails sneeze from time to time because they're allergic to the spray required by the airport regulations: **Every little hair in place and the decent appearance of female personnel will not be put in doubt.** The nurses fasten on the chastity belt before taking up the littleoldlady; Penelope, unconscious, richer than rich, has revived too late. The porter has gone off whistling with her purse. Penelope has an unbearable need to go to the bathroom and, with the power money brings, just lets go then and there without apologies. One of the blondes will put on rubber gloves and clean the floor almost without wrinkling her new little upturned nose, pride of the surgeons.
—Señora Penelope, is there some family member we could call?
—Family member, no. A radio program. And a TV station.
—Are you famous? They always told me that working in a hospital even if only as a nurse and not as a doctor would give me access to the last moments of some important person and then I'd be

well known myself. It's unfair how these things work. Here I am. Agile. Slim. Tall. Young. And here you are.
   Old
      squat
         bum heart
            semi-incontinent she was heard to say to the young intern   semi-incontinent he said   she doesn't do it to annoy you it's that she can't control herself and those boys know what they're talking about because they're not yet alcoholic, they don't yet have the wherewithal to pay for the luxuries that lead doctors astray; they have unpretentious lovers who demand nothing of them, nights when no one is looking they're satisfied with patting a girl's bottom and nothing more because they study all the time, go out with their little sweethearts and lovers once a week and have to go to bed early because they're on call the next day, so if he said it that's how it is

very unfair, Penelope, that you should be famous and not me —You're too envious for your age. I've seen people whose hair actually turned green because of such feelings. And anyway, I'm not incontinent. It was for convenience, so they wouldn't take me away, but now I'm fine, I don't need to pile up debts. I don't want to hand out so many tips to you. They say you do it because it's your duty, because the hospital requires it but I've seen how they treat the ones who come without jewels and little cultivated pearl buttons, without mink, without leather luggage. They treat them like dirt. Give them beds in shared rooms and never never give them a bed by the window. Me, on the other hand, you should see how they pamper me because you can tell my position by my clothes and in an airport I'm taken care of, but don't imagine I feel as strong as a bull now and am leaving to find my sweet sweetheart; the radio listeners must be biting their nails with all the money that's been bet. They tell me some retired people hand over their pensions directly to the radio station and that's nothing compared to the amounts taken in as television bets. It's very complicated because to me Rita looks more and more whorish, don't you notice she's gained weight and her fleshy mouth and curves look somewhat pawed over?

  a thin virgin girl

    a decent girl

      that no one wants to touch

and from night to morning those folds and creases

  I have my suspicions, my dear nurse

don't you think a woman should keep her dignity

  until she's fully grown?

  no fooling around for me at that age

I like how she listens to my ditty. Her patience charms me. Yes, you do merit a tip. You arouse my need to share my fortune. Will you hand me my purse? They must have put it in the closet, next to my clothes.

—There's no purse there. We already looked for it yesterday to identify you, nobody knows your surname; we knew your given name was Penelope because of your silver bracelet. It must have been a present from when you were poor because I have one just like it that I bought for myself. . . .

—What do you mean, there's no purse? Stop screwing around or I'll have you searched from head to toe.

—As you like, Señora Penelope. Don't get upset because the next time you may not make it back from the heart attack.

I'm so picky, won't take something just because it's there

The porter trails through the corridors of the Institute. The porter has a mission. He's walked for hours. Has blisters on his feet. Trails along being licked by the lubricious skunks. His body is well camouflaged against the green-black marble of the floor. He doesn't want to be seen. He's still shivering from the flu he caught during the rainy season. He's happy. Under cover, the purse has become glued to his armpit and nobody would suspect he was hiding anything beneath his uniform. Out of breath, worn out, he sees through the peephole an imposing group of ugly women during the daily assembly before the authorities. He listens to the speeches of the director and the deputy director, almost sneezes because of the smell of urine when the women turn around and let flow the mark of their disdain but feels a sense of well-being. He's arrived. At last. One of them would be his choice. He'd be able to show he was an upstanding man. They'd buy a Swiss chalet and be photographed in the doorway, with a background of waterfalls and mountains. His future wife was here.

The porter's name was Juan. He realizes he needs a traditional woman, one like they used to be, and what could be better than to go to the Institute and buy himself a proper one. Rounded up. Interned. My ugly one, he would whisper tenderly into her ear. At home day and night under penalty of being detained again. Such a woman is worth her weight in gold. Such a woman justifies a chance robbery whose astronomical sum would save him ten years of lifting wallets in the baggage claim as the travelers bend over to pick up the heavy suitcases full of smuggled goods. Such a woman would be ashamed to show herself naked. Such a woman would admire his masturbating sessions before the mirror. Such a woman is necessary because the Academy has become very expensive and Juan is a farsighted man who wishes to get in on the ground floor before others realize that the Institute can be an excellent source of supply. With the littleoldlady's money perhaps he can buy two women. With the littleoldlady's money any woman whatsoever can be pretty but he will not point it out because on top of being farsighted he's a man who likes to keep secrets like all men who go around dressed in gray. Juan searches and searches for someone in the Institute who will sell him a couple of women. But before, of course, he has to choose.

me too

—I feel much better after the naps. You're right, Rogelio. Forgive me for all I said earlier.
—Don't mention it
—No, really. Imagine it took not seeing you during the rainy season to realize I missed you and I don't say that only because of the show. You know I adore seeing you do rolls and tumbles but if you think hypnosis is a better treatment . . .
—It's not a matter of seems to me. You can see the difference. Even in your hair. Look at the curls. They're soft, they don't look like gilded wire the way they used to. It's something else. They even make one want to touch them
—go ahead
—Like this . . . see, they're soft and your face also
—Rain has moisturizing properties
—As for my salary I believe the time has come to raise it in accord with my new duties.
—What new duties do you mean?
—To sleep beside you after the sessions of hypnosis are over. Don't forget I like to move around, jump, I have to control my nervous tics. And then, there's my project. I must save a considerable sum.
—Not another word. You'll get your raise, Rogelio. If you wish you can move in here and save the cost of rent.
—No, Camila, I thank you with all my heart; I'll keep on sleeping in the circus. After all, that's the most secure job I have and I think we're done with the rainy season.

Camila has taken on a cowlike expression. Her eyes, empty before, have an almost melancholy look, and around the mouth the hint of a smile reveals the girl with the braces in the photograph. Rogelio knew that look very well. As a young man he'd seen it on faces of women who came to learn to dance under the pretext of an upcoming party and afterwards waited for him, eager for an intense and furtive encounter. Rogelio shied away from them at first because he preferred going with Josefina, but once he was married, the extra hour of income became indispensable and he soon had a harem of women and girls fighting over him in a free-for-all like the public auctions that proliferated in that neighborhood.

—You never told me why you needed so much money.

—It's because I realize I'm in love, have been in love all my life, and I need to rescue someone.

—At your age?

—Don't criticize me. What's happening to you is worse; without my treatment you wouldn't have the faintest hope of becoming seductive and interesting. . . .

—Rogelio, would you like to go to the movies with me? We could have tea in a pastry shop before and afterward supper in a restaurant. All my treat, naturally. If you wish, I'll pay you double time since ideally we should do it on a weekend.

—As a matter of fact, it would be good practice for you, Camila, but I'm busy. Various things are pending that I have to take care of, the accounting . . .

—So then you don't need cash so urgently.

—Yes, I need it, but on a weekend . . .

—Triple. I'll pay triple.

Rogelio adjusted his tie, smoothed his hair dyed black, gave Camila a pinch on the cheek, and said good-bye, not mentioning when he'd return. He walked with a sure step, the nervous tics gone. He was thinking that soon he'd have enough money to bribe the night watchman and kidnap Josefina. *My sweetheart*, he heard Camila say in a whisper, and if someone could have seen her, they would have sworn a tear sprang to her eye.

never stopping
   never ceasing
      the hormones
here comes the revolution

The minions of the cell circle around the table Indian file. They know they have a major mess on their hands. They know Teresa has fucked them up with the robbery and how. They know somebody has goofed. They blame each other. Obviously, if we admit lesbians, corruption is bound to spread because they've slept with one of us, there's not the slightest doubt,
   if we admit females in love with themselves
         if we admit women who masturbate
cooks
   lovers of their bosses
single mothers
   widows
or women married to men they adore
if we admit, well, any woman whatsoever, we run a risk, they can deceive us they can pull the wool over our eyes   they can kill us off like chicks for the grill

   sisters:
   the moment has come to go underground
   the moment has come to take up arms
   let's not allow anyone to join us
   let's be a clandestine unit
   let's speak in dialect
   let's not make propaganda

let's swear   let's swear eternal loyalty to the cell   let's use disguises so no one will recognize us let's go regularly to the meetings   let's plan the persecution and punishment of Teresa (boos and hisses from cell members at the mention of her name)
   we have an enemy   we're strong   we're unique
   we'll fix her

The woman making the speech was wearing a gray uniform that came down to her heels, a sort of coverall of an old rough texture. She wore buttoned shoes and on her head a kerchief that covered most of her face. In a hoarse smoker's voice she said it was for religious reasons. They believed her. They let her stay anonymous according to the cell's new rules of confidentiality. They respected her secret and made her into their leader. The revolutionaries were desperate because they couldn't understand Teresa's hypocrisy. This austere woman, on the other hand, with no flighty notions about beauty, was the cell's ideal, the new independent woman capable of throwing even the Institute personnel off the track because her garb made her unclassifiable. At last the perfect woman for present times. *She hides herself as a strategy and not out of shyness* some said; others said *what luck to have someone like her to guide us in this search   a disinterested person   a person with ideals   and to think she didn't even know that treacherous bitch Teresa.* You, on the other hand, will have realized that this woman is none other than Rafa, who's trying to find Teresa to punish her, impeach her. Let her pay, Rafa said to himself every time, disguise in place, he started off to the meetings of the cell.

choose quick
    grab the chance

The members of the little cabal are feverish. They've come down with the measles. Red faces, arms a bit swollen, they're complaining. They're young. Want their mamas. Clamor for orange juice. Nights they scratch and try to spy the coming of daylight, sleepless, exhausted. The doctor of the Institute is unable to cope. He'd thought of letting the disease run its course, as in the case of Marisita, who's now walking, erect and pale, holding Josefina's arm. But he can't because the inspection team is coming in the next two days and if everything's not in order their profitable contract won't be renewed. His wife has already packed their bags for the summer vacation in the union hotel; his daughters have had all their body hair removed to be ready for the nude beach. Danilo knows the measles would be over in ten days but he has to act quickly. From one day to the next. In the basement of the Institute he prepares potions, mixes diuretics with amphetamines; upset by how insipid his concoctions are, he tests and discards. Head swimming from the experiments, he doesn't notice Juan, who, worn out, is resting beside the basket where the skunks are also sleeping. Juan wakes up first and, hidden by a pillar, follows each one of Danilo's movements as he tests cosmetics, paints, because Danilo has made up his mind: he'll have to conceal the spots, pull an ephemeral veil over the reddened bodies while the inspection lasts. When Danilo, wrapped in a sheet, tests to see if the paint will stain clothing, he stumbles and falls over a skunk, frightening it so it takes off running and trips Juan, revealing his hiding place.
—Juan García, at your service
—Dr. Danilo . . . well, the surname doesn't matter. Better to leave things that way. What are you doing here?
This is an institute strictly outside the scrutiny of the public at large. I know all the employees, so don't start telling me some lie, tell the truth and I'll leave you in peace, because I don't care if these experiments get around.
—Don't worry about me. I only want to find one or two wives.

Maybe you can help me. Young but ugly. I want her to stay at home wait for me
 so I'll be the only man in her life
  so she'll be grateful to me
a woman who doesn't need to be entertained. I'll buy her a friend just like herself and they can keep each other company. . . .

—You're crazy, Juan. Any woman you pick up on the street can make herself ugly with a little effort and attention. You don't have to come to the Institute for that. A slight change of diet.

—The pickups turn arrogant. You have to praise them all the time, it's tiring; I've gone through several but don't get me started. . . .

—How much are you prepared to pay? Keep in mind there are extra expenses because they call the roll every day, each one has a number, and there's the cost of falsifying application forms, tape recorders with tapes to imitate the voice, a salary for someone to unmake the beds where your two usually slept. It's not a minor thing, it's a big deal.

Danilo was exaggerating because the authorities were so distracted and overwhelmed by the ups and downs of their own business affairs that they paid little or no attention to the swarm of internees. The population of the Institute had grown to an incredible extent in the past months. The rain, full of chemicals damaging to permanents and rinses, had wrecked the hairdos of the entire feminine population and the lines of the detained were growing with no end in sight. Husbands, boyfriends, oversexed cousins accepted the fact of separation and turned to painting, composing boleros, and selling chocolates.

—Look, I have a purse here. You count the money in it and after I choose you tell me if it's enough. . . .

—But this is a ladies' purse. You've robbed somebody. I can't compromise myself this way. You must understand that a man of my position in society has to be careful about appearances. Just because you find me in the basement due to the timing of the inspection doesn't mean I'm about to help cover up a robbery. . . . —Cover up, no, I haven't said how I got the purse. There's no question of coverup. And remember what I tell you, I won the purse and its contents in the lottery. You won't cover up but you'll clean up and I get what I want. With the understanding that you don't help me choose, I need to concentrate because it's an important decision. A young one and an old one. You give me a doctor's outfit and I'll walk through the wards.

Juan had achieved Rogelio's greatest ambition. Nights he walked through the wards with total freedom. He could take any internee away with him. Including Josefina. Danilo was making plans for an independent existence in a country with a cold climate and with snow that would fall in round symmetrical flakes and line the streets like foreign-exchange figures in the orderly national budget of that advanced nation. Nothing common for me, Danilo said to himself. He believed he had it in him to be an elegant, sensitive gentleman. Soon he'd buy a cane. His wife and daughters would never know how happy he'd be to leave them, after enduring their tyranny. Let them be poor. Let them beg. Or better yet, let them be put in the Institute so they can be carried off by some porter. The money made the blood race in his veins. He was sick of summers at the beach, poker games, eating steak with french fries. Danilo saw his soul. It was greenback-green and beat as strongly as any heart.

A. M. A. R.

In the Academy of Housewives where the Otherwoman had made herself a millionaire without turning arrogant, impotent husbands and frigid boyfriends had coffee and doughnuts, played poker, and now paid scant attention to the dutiful women who collected their nail clippings, massaged their calluses, and cooked stews with bacon. The Otherwoman was not detained because she was not only smart but also clever at keeping records. She had photographs of each one of the Academy's clients on file
    had made an album
        charted descending curves of virility
    recorded whimpers of *mommy give me a little more soup* uttered by generals, public figures, weight lifters, loan sharks
    accumulated
        classified
            put under lock and key
a bland, gelatinous urban fresco where the most macho men came only to turn into schoolboys around snack time. The Otherwoman had managed to transform her Academy into a lively and expensive café. The fact that they'd begun to detain her employees was a boon for her because she didn't have to pay them any compensation whatsoever. At night, a few calls to the emergency service of the Institute and immediately she got what she wanted:
—Hello, may I speak to a supervisor, please.
—One moment . . .
(while the connection was being made, you could hear tapes of Caribbean music that the director and the deputy directory had brought back from their vacations)
—How may I help you?
—This city is getting worse and worse. You people have the job of maintaining the aesthetic quality of the place. Here in the Office of Tourism we're unable to keep up with the complaints. In my neighborhood there's a woman who goes out every day at **nine o'clock in the morning** when there's a lot of coming and going in

hotels and shops of the area; she goes swiveling an ass of truly enormous proportions. We're used to it but the average tourist wants to see women with good figures so they can go back home and say: Here you can eat better than in any other place but there the women are something else; I've seen many and every one of them could make you dream for centuries. How do those foreign women stay in such good shape? It must be something in the water, the landscape, the beaches, dietetic products, the clothes, something indefinable, but something that we could buy and take home as a souvenir, and if not, we can come back next year with a group of friends or clients, plan a longer visit. As you see, my complaint goes to the crux of the matter. If you people don't do your job, the country goes under, because let's not fool ourselves, the biggest industry is tourism.

At this point, the Otherwoman would clear her throat, wait for the supervisor on duty on the other end of the line to get prepared for a threat, and then in a conciliatory tone would assure him that if he'd take down the address of that woman and a few others she'd seen on the streets in different parts of the city, she wouldn't denounce him to the executive committee. That invariably got their attention and was the way she got rid of ninety-seven-point-five percent of her employees. With the others—a rickets-ridden Indian woman dressed in navy blue, the ex-bearded-woman of the circus who could no longer bear the jealous scenes Camila threw every night since she'd realized she'd fallen in love at last and with none other than than Rogelio, and a peroxide blonde with the voice of a canary whose hair and forehead had turned green because of the poor-quality dyes they'd begun to use in the beauty salon since Teresa escaped with the funds meant for importing beauty products—the Otherwoman converted the Academy into a café with a pool table in the back. The men understood now that what they really wanted was to be with each other and they paid huge sums so the Otherwoman would prohibit the entrance of women with a stern notice:

A. M. A. R.

ACADEMY FOR MEN:
ACTIVITIES AND RECREATION

The Otherwoman is clever. Has bank accounts in Switzerland. Has no need to spend money on clothes or make-up
    The Otherwoman could be free
        at peace
            one day could have a gilded jacuzzi installed in the middle of the dining room   drink piña coladas in the Bahamas with millionaire arms dealers   drug lords   producers of elixir
    The Otherwoman could be high-flying and amoral   like a raptor or a sparrow if she didn't have a thorn, a curiosity, something she cudgeled her brain with night and day, **she is,** we know, we sense it by the way she looks at him when he returns from Camila's house and when he comes out changed for the circus, by her worry that he might catch cold, she's **in love with Rogelio**, her neighbor. Up to the eyeballs.

all or nothing at all

Rogelio has saved a sum of money that will allow him to get into the Institute tonight to see if Josefina recognizes him. He tries sentences like Hi, *of course you remember me, my treasure, love of my life, woman of my dreams.* Or more sincere: *I know you've forgotten me but I can't go on this way. I'm sorry I let them take you away but you gave no signs of recognizing me and I thought, better the Institute than the insane asylum.* But here he stops. He wants a more forceful apology. A true, dense memory. An event. Something real without words that will return her to when they met in the School of Dance. All this is very problematical, my gentle sentimental readers, because Rogelio is really still looking for the woman of the doorknob, but he knows, is well aware that he'll only be able to reinvent her and open the door when Josefina's sleeping beside him in the bed.

Meanwhile, Camila has changed. Her curls are soft, the hypnotic exercises with Rogelio have made her wish to go out alone, leave herself open to chance. It's night in the city. Not too much traffic due to the shortage of gasoline brought on by the crisis in the producing countries. Camila walks at random. Stumbles over a bundle and realizes it's a woman with a purple bruise on her cheek. Elena, startled, wakes up, covering her face to protect herself:

—No, I'm not going to harm you. Don't worry. Did you fall? How did you get that? Or is it a tattoo? Let me see, don't cover it up, I want to see. Yes, it looks like a tattoo of a very tiny hand. It resembles a bruise but it must be a tattoo, right? I adore these stylish innovations. I myself am a woman in a phase of transformation. Look, earlier I was, I don't know, on the other side. For a long time. And later, just like that, by chance, in the circus, I met an extraordinary therapist, a man of limitless scientific depth, who, through dance and hypnosis, has left me ready to live. I would love to impress him. I would like, well, you know . . .

—Yes, because I'm a fortuneteller.

—A fortuneteller! And why are you like this, sleeping in the street?

I thought fortunetellers could get whatever they wanted. There's one, without going further afield, who has a booth near here and you should see the lines, people who want her to tell their fortunes. Men. Women. Everybody. Up to now I've never gone because hardly anything has ever happened to me and above all I was interested in exploring my family history but the minute I'm on the same wave length as everybody else, I'll get in line too. Tomorrow, for example. To talk to her about you and ask her if we're going to meet again.

—Tomorrow she won't be there.

—Why do you say these things to me? You must be offended because of the business of the tattoo, you don't want to share the secret. I understand you now. We're strangers. But we could become friends. For instance, right now I invite you to have a beer in a German bar two blocks from here.

—When we enter a waiter with dandruff will bend over your glass and let the flakes fall into the foam; they'll stay hidden but two hours later you'll feel terrible stomach cramps and you'll vomit everything you've eaten including the dandruff. But at least the next day you'll be as good as new. Maybe you want to go anyway.

—You're trying to make me sad, dampen my hopes, screw up my life; tell me the secret of the little hand on your cheek and I'll go. But . . . why are you bloody? Is that a hospital gown you're wearing?

—I'm Elena, the fortuneteller you're looking for. I just had a baby and left the hospital as soon as possible but I couldn't get very far because they did a Cesarean. If you wish, you can help me; so the upshot is what I foresaw about the beer must have changed your mind about going to that bar.

—And you'll tell me the secret of the little hand? I'm sure it would fascinate Rogelio. I want him to look at me day and night. I'm going to have mine made yellow, not purple, because purple looks like a slap. Although that might even please Rogelio. I'll buy a

whip, put on a black garter belt, lie in the chair, he will tie me up. It would be nice if Rogelio would have fantasies about me. . . .
—Don't waste your money. Rogelio is busy. Rogelio has a mission. Look, I can't go on like this because it really hurts. . . . Will you call an ambulance? But have them take me to another hospital. . . .
—You know Rogelio?

Elena had fainted by the time the ambulance arrived. Despite Camila's protests they took her back to the same hospital, but at least Camila succeeded in not having her put near the delivery rooms. Even so, the nurses identified Elena and told Camila the story of Amanda's birth. Camila was so enchanted with life. A friend and a baby. A family. For several days and nights she sat beside Elena, waiting for the infection to subside; it was making her delirious and causing her to spill the secrets of the future of half the city. Camila listened carefully with her newly acquired memory. She wanted to get to the part where Rogelio confused her with the woman with the doorknob but Elena was cured before that happened and, with eyes open and affectionate, said to Camila: *I believe I foresee that you have the soul of a mother, would you like to adopt my baby, Amanda? She's a love, a true gift of nature and I believe has an affectionate soul like yours; a mama with golden curls will fill her with happiness. If you wish, I'll pay you a monthly fee.*

3
back and forth they go

to each his own

Dear radio listeners:

                We must inform you that the broadcast *Engagements of Yesteryear* has come to an end. We are grateful to you for the bets received and we assure you the minute we know the whereabouts of the littleoldlady, our elderly heroine in search of the strong young romeo with whom she has carried on extensive telephone conversations, we will let you know the outcome of the romance that has kept us all on edge and hopeful.

    I share with all of you the desire that both will find happiness. I do not blame those who have bet on a crime, those holding a pessimistic point of view regarding human relations, who maintain that he will rob her of her money, abandon her in front of an oncoming train, or poison her to avoid future problems. I join with those who see in her enterprise a sign of new romantic feelings, a return to our dearest customs of conquest and seduction. It is a matter of a new era, with no barriers of age or sex. Women, represented by our brave elderly lady, have taken the initiative. Good night, esteemed, beloved, generous radio listeners. We will return when the team of detectives that we have employed finds our impassioned pair.

    Fernando had taped the announcement broadcast on the radio before setting sail for Thailand, carrying with him the money collected in the bets. An ex-policeman, who charged a special fee on condition that he not be denounced on the radio for being a torturer, had followed the littleoldlady to the very hospital where she was recovering at that moment. He had orders to kill her on foreign territory so the crime would be harder to solve, but when he saw her fall in the airport with a heart attack, he thought he could escape without having to lend his name to the affair. He had bad luck. The littleoldlady made a miraculous recovery. The hospital's technical and scientific staff threw a party in her honor. They found her appealing despite her looney ideas. The littleoldlady was grateful to them because they'd treated her for free, and since she didn't have a penny to her name, the only way she could think of to reciprocate was to work as a volunteer until the debt was paid. The ex-policeman got bored watching her and with a sigh of resignation and relief went back to the city where hordes of radio listeners and TV viewers milling around in front of the broadcasting studios had created a continuous and indignant vigil.

  WE'RE RETIREES
  WE'RE COOKS
HUSBANDS HOUSEWIVES CHILDREN EXECUTIVES MANAGERS
  WE ARE POLITICIANS
EMPLOYEES   CUCKOLDS   FIANCÉS   VIRGINS
VICTIMS
HEALTHY   SICK   COWARDLY   BRAVE

ALL SWINDLED
  WE WANT REVENGE
WE WANT RESTITUTION
  HERE NOTHING HAS HAPPENED
LET'S GO BACK TO THE BEGINNING   LET'S NOT BET ON ANYBODY'S FUTURE

It was out of hand. The authorities didn't know what to do. All involved in the bets. All screwed. Fernando, a potentate in Thailand, had become untouchable in a matter of weeks given his high rank in the international traffic of children and women. Who would dare go against his army? Surely not these humble people of the city with no other resources to offer than its crooked ways and a handful of speculators, hustlers, retirees, unemployed, and schoolteachers with red-painted nails. The people didn't want to leave. They were waiting. Waiting for somebody to make the announcement on television, because they believed nothing they hadn't seen on their TV screens. They'd only heard the news on the radio. A mere headline in the newspapers. Rita had not said a word to them. No trace of Rita. The baskets of sweet treats, the telegrams, the anonymous threats seemed to have fallen into the most complete void.

Heriberto's apprenticeship training had made her more feisty. In the early days she had followed him like a puppy, with the same expression she'd shown when she worked beside Tota. *My shadow, my humid little shadow, my hot-water bottle, my jello, my whore, my red-hot sweetheart, mommy,* Heriberto said to her, and she, roly-poly, did nothing more than lick her lips and ask for instructions, but a few sessions before the camera with the leading man with the enormous genitals were enough for her to realize that Heriberto was lacking something. *Don't come to me with any more requests because the business doesn't interest me,* she said one day and Heriberto saw his world of happiness crumble. The fleshy mouth, the little teeth softened by chocolates and lollypops, all that would be a thing of the past. Heriberto felt more fear than disgust, that's why in a supplicating tone of voice he let Rita know

    that this was not what he expected from a woman who'd been a virgin

    that she shouldn't worry about the future

    that her frustration could lead to suicide

    that she owed everything she knew to him

    that she'd cry her eyes out from grief

    that he'd lost the red glove in a bet

—I'll never forgive you for the glove. From now on I'll produce my own movies. Without the glove our engagement is finished. Go. I'm in a hurry. I have to talk with my TV viewers.

Rita had caught on to her commercial value and had signed a contract with an international distributor giving her a generous percentage of the tickets sold for her pictures. She was actress, producer, and director. In a few brief minutes Heriberto ceased to exist as far as she was concerned. Perhaps because of his professorial manner or his flabby muscles due to lack of physical training or the modest size of his genitals in comparison with the leading man's, her partner in the movies; the thing is Rita was a free woman for the first time, a professional with no ties.

Heriberto followed her for half a block while she, flaunting her hips, concentrated on putting on the pink-tinted make-up that gave her the cherubic air admired so much by the TV viewers sitting on their sofas.

—Darling, you're crazy. You're tired. So many rehearsals. So much fucking in front of the camera. I promise you time off, an early retirement, summer vacations at a spa. I promise to fire that vulgar actor, that butcher with no manners or conversation, and I'll look for another one who'll entertain you, who can talk in an interesting way, a newspaperman, a Ph.D. in literature, a graduate of the School of Education.

—Don't talk to me. The glove had a function, a secret, an elegance. If you don't have it, I don't need you. Besides, I no longer want you to find leading men for me, I'll manage by myself. I'll go out into the street and find a cheap hungry one, I'll hire him by the day, I'll feed him with the presents the TV viewers send and that's it. Economical, practical, and profitable.

At that moment Heriberto began to feel nausea rising in his throat. First he vomited an apple in little green and yellow pieces, then a greenish liquid, and only later, like a miracle, out came whole, though greasy, the red glove. Rita didn't see it because she took to her heels at the first heave. She wanted to talk to her public, tell them that everything would turn out all right.   Crowded in front of the station were some who'd already bloodied their hands from banging on the doors so hard. Women who'd left their husbands after discovering they'd bet their salaries on the sly, mothers and fathers who'd spent the small legacies intended for their children, workers who'd bribed half the universe to try their luck. You've guessed it: they were an enterprising people willing to accept the risks necessary to better their fortune but now, knowing they'd been swindled, they wanted to make sure, to hear it from some person in authority who might save them from the whirlpool threatening to drown them.

Rita, calm and smiling, looked them in the eyes without pretending anything profound. She measured each face that approached her, viewers moved at seeing her in person. Rita, the star of every wager, the bubbly greedy daily dinner guest, did not lack resources. She stopped, stood on a garbage can, put her right arm over her eyes, and when she was sure that everyone realized who she was and you could touch the silence, she began to cry. First slowly to capture their attention, then uncontrollably. The demonstrators, moved and grateful for this show of solidarity with their plight, began to console her. Some invited her to their homes, to weekend country places, to a volleyball game, a trip with recent graduates to Calamuchita, but Rita didn't stop crying until a Finnish banker approached her and said: *Make the speech now, my girl - very soon we'll leave in a whirl.*

It was love at first sight, at first sound. The banker's intuition excited Rita; her spirit and the left half of her abdomen tensed up. We'll be business partners, she assured him, wiping away the last snot with the silk handkerchief he handed her, and with a noble glance turned to the crowd.

mother love

Camila immediately decided she'd move Amandita to her house. Elena had told her nothing about where the slap had come from; it would remain on her cheek, indelible, until years later when she'd have a peeling done, leaving her with Swedish-type cheekbones. Curls falling carelessly over her forehead, Camila began a day of frenetic shopping: teddy bears, cute summer outfits, a communion dress on sale, a china doll, two rattles (one red, another with blue-and-yellow dots), milk, milk, and more milk, custard, a mirror, a smock because, given how precocious Amanda was, she was certain to go to school very soon. Now in the house she searched high and low until she opened a dusty little box and found the orthodontic braces she'd worn in her favorite photo. *Amandita will have everything, she'll also pose like a well-cared-for child of an upper-middle- or perhaps lower-middle-class family, because now with the installment plan you never know what sort of people you're dealing with: when she wears a shiny orthodontic brace, they'll know she has someone who takes good care of her; she'll dedicate the photo to me, and all her sweethearts will see it and say how expensive the braces must have been, and they'll say what luck to have a mommy like that, so dedicated, how I wish I'd been treated that way, and Amandita, now grown, will say that of her two mommies there's only one she truly loves, the one who gave her her biggest treasures, and so we'll go to the matinée movies all together until her boyfriend sees how attractive, intelligent, and mature I am, and somewhat timidly at first but with sudden passion he declares his love for me. How could that be. My daughter comes first of all, I must not allow you to look at me in such a way or let you put your hand under my blouse, imagine that although I'm not a married woman, these things bother me, taint the dignity of my history. It's here when he'll tell me he knows I'm not Amanda's real mother, that he never believed the story and in any case I'm too young to have a teenage daughter like Amanda calling me mama. Now in bed he'll sing me a zarzuela of his love for me with all the high notes, nothing has happened between Amanda and me, he'll say, we're not going to get married, we won't go to the racetrack on Sundays leaving you alone in front of the*

TV, we won't have children or ever see each other again because I've discovered the true path of my passion in this bed, in these curls; it was that orthodontic brace, that welcoming smile; it was, I now know, only a premonition of our happiness. It's then we'll double-lock the door so Amanda can no longer get in this house. Let her go live with Elena, visit her and see her and tell her problems to her, if by any chance she calls her mommy, if by any chance she admires her Swedish cheekbones. Never again in this house, let her leave me alone with my sweetheart; mommies urgently need to live, after all; if not, why get dressed, all decked out, fix curls. Camila was happy making her preparations. Finally she had succeeded in getting the neighbors to talk to her, they were full of emotion because she was going to take in a baby girl abandoned by her mother. Why have children? they asked her with a lilting complicity, why if they didn't want to take care of them. What luck that child has. To have found her. To have run across such a charitable soul. Camila was not surprised when Rogelio missed his appointment that afternoon because she was also very busy. Enough of naps and hypnosis; she wanted to be awake.

I'll turn out the light the better to think of you . . .

—Filomena, the moment has come for you to talk to me a little. Don't you realize if you don't move your lips now and then, you can be left with that grimace on your face forever? Imagine for a woman of the jungle like yourself. You need to move the jawbone so you can eat those very hard fruits just plucked from the trees, crush coconuts with the shell on, because I'm sure you don't use our methods. Filomena, fine if what I suggest as jungle food doesn't please you, I'll take you to a restaurant. I'll escape from here and take you to a restaurant. Did I tell you how it was I got married to Rogelio? I get the impression you like me to tell you our story. I'll happily keep on telling you but when you stare at me with such hard unblinking eyes it disturbs me. Look, the question of time difference shouldn't be so great although, of course, since you were kidnapped by Indians from around there, you're confused and think I'm out to harm you. If that's what you believe, you're very mistaken. I've been waiting for you so we can go wherever you choose. For us it'll be easy because I know they're afraid of us, they don't know how to treat us, and any little thing we'll pretend to be crazy and they'll send us to the insane asylum. There I can get you all kinds of remedies; it's more amusing there because they put on a real show. I know these things because I ask for information in exchange for my songs. You understand, my dear?

    I have a gift
even without trying
I have a gift
that brings me lots of dough
    a little gift I've got
red hot
    a mammoth gift that goes ding-dong
in my song

how tired you must be, Filomena, because when I dance like this all the other women join me and we end up on top of one another laughing our heads off, most of all the little band of plotters, who need affection and caresses because they're so young, and that consoles them for the life they can't lead outside. They plot, poor things, but they don't know why. They like to have secrets, a club, to play with those skunks more germ-ridden all the time. The thing is, my dear Filomena, you frighten me somewhat today, you're so tense. I'll turn out the light so I can't see that glitter in your eyes, it seems you're going to spring at me or something like that, like a cat or a panther. Better this way, in the dark. Rogelio was never a hard worker but he went to an office where he kept busy with men's affairs. Budgets. Forms. Answering the telephone. It made him feel more like a husband, I believe. To have a job like the others. But I saw he had a tremor in his legs, a kind of nervous tic at night whenever we practiced a particular dance number so we wouldn't get out of the routine because it was the most secure part of our marriage, I never ever told him that I no longer liked dancing with him, no longer recognized in his steps the Rogelio of the School of Dance, the one I waited for between classes. Look, we probably could have danced and gone on dancing, I think that technically we could have entered various competitions, joined the circus, gone to Russia with the troupe from the cell, but we never got the courage to leave the neighborhood. You understand, when you know where to buy your favorite fruit, fresh meat, newly baked bread, you can't move. We were so happy. If it hadn't been for that almost imperceptible tic, I swear I would've talked to my Rogelio, would've said, Darling, my matador, my flamenco lover, my leading man, I'll help you find the doorknob. If it hadn't been for that tic, I would recognize you in any darkness and finally, with words, signs, caresses, would've greeted you in fine fashion.

I've been looking in all the wrong places

The littleoldlady had not given up the idea of finding her sweetheart of yesteryear. She had a map of the country in her room, and whenever she finished her chores at the hospital, she started the tape recorder and began to study the accents of different regions. She'd kept all the conversations broadcast on the radio; with the help of the hospital's phonetics experts she succeeded in reconstructing the block where the final vowel of each word was accented as he did; *my timid little sweetheart* she called him sometimes. O Timoteo, as she nicknamed him to ease the communication with the Romanian linguist who was charting the genealogy of his voice. After several months he was able to construct an exact profile of the individual. Knew his address, name, occupation. The hospital provided her with a list of his vaccinations and the results of his most recent blood tests. These days one had to be sure. Such an individual could have the sickness; **at your age**, they told her in worried tones, at your age you should be careful. Don't kiss. Don't touch. Don't look deeply into each other's eyes. The hospital's ideal of love was of a gleaming cleanliness; the littleoldlady didn't even have an ideal of love. She was curious, wanted to amuse herself among the fortuitous events of life. You all sense she has no wish to be immortal; she was a woman of intense life experiences who'd paid her dues and reached her goals. She never let on to anyone she was disillusioned. She'd thought the sweetheart of yesteryear would be someone with a developed personality, enigmatic, with a certain charisma. Instead, she'd discovered the one who'd so captivated her on the telephone was a plain porter. Juan, how am I going to call him Juan? The same name as the man at the dry cleaners. Impossible. Let him keep on being Timoteo. Not only that, he lied to me. He's not engaged, he's not even married. He's weak, and without a cent to his name. She didn't tell anyone how she felt because she loved being involved in the venture. What interested her was winning. To be photographed with the porter, be recognized by the radio listeners and the TV viewers as one more gutsy lady. Camera in hand, the littleoldlady walks toward the modest apartment where she might have found Juan if he hadn't been at that very moment at the Institute with Danilo.

—Let's go very slowly and I'll let you see my little sick ones first, Juan. While we look them over, you choose one of them. Or did you say two? You're not going to take two with measles. . . .
—It seems to me the best would be to take one young one and one old one.
—I advise you to procure two of the same generation, neighborhood, social class, and high school, because if not, once they're outside they won't become friends and will insist on talking to you day and night. They'll keep you awake with the problems of their relationship. They'll want you to be the referee. Your house will turn into an arena for an international soccer championship meet. Listen to me. A woman needs entertainment and if you have to provide it for two or even just for one, you won't be able to do anything else.
—No, you don't know what you're talking about. Two women of the same age with the same characteristics are dangerous for a man like me; they'll spend their time gossiping, setting traps for me to fall into every single day. And behind my back, while one pretends to help me, the other will wink an eye and they'll make fun of me. Their pleasure will be more intense because of their ugliness and they'll turn my house into a spot for deceitful games. No. Let them keep each other company, yes. Friendship, what is called deep friendship, no. That's dangerous, leads to conspiracies, upsets the balance of things.
—Whatever you want, let's hurry because these girls will be waking up soon and with the itching who knows what sort of mood they'll be in.

Together Juan and Danilo walk through the corridors of the Institute. Juan marvels at the number of women interned, is filled

with hope because the present overcrowding will make his house a paradise for the ones he chooses. Actually he wants most of all to be happy. Rejected by all the pretty girls of his neighborhood because of the striking mole that covered his lower lip, Juan found refuge in the *Engagements of Yesteryear* and a good supplement to his ludicrous salary as porter. The littleoldlady had led him into a tense, emotional quagmire. He could've kept talking to her for centuries. He loved her voice. It fascinated him to think of her gray hair, her glasses with tortoise-shell frames, the purse beneath her arm like the one of the woman he robbed in the airport. The littleoldlady made his heart flutter, drink coffee after hours, brush his teeth like mad before talking with her on the phone. No matter how hard he brushed or how much sweeter his breath was, the mole stayed there with its dark message, a letter sent by some ancestor by way of his body. That's why he lied to the littleoldlady when she wanted to come to see him, that's why he turned down the chance to lead a life of leisure on some tropical island where he could fan her and serve her eggnog in tiny cups with gold rims. Juan studies Danilo; he feels resentful; Danilo's way of talking makes Juan feel inferior but he remembers he's the one with the money to pay for Danilo's services and takes a deep breath and asks if he can't enter a room whose closed door suggests a decisive encounter.
—That room? No. I suggest you not go in there. I don't even dare to go in; I'm dead serious.
—If it's because that's where you keep the most monstrous ones, then I'd be extremely interested in going in, don't forget this is not a beauty contest. Quite the opposite . . .
—It's something worse, more difficult to deal with. My advice is to keep going. I have plans for investing the money I earn from this transaction, I need to pack my bags, transfer funds. Please, don't make me lose time.
—I don't care if it turns out to cost more. I don't want just any

ugly woman who with a few bucks and cosmetics may change her looks and then drop me; if monsters are available that's exactly what I want, women that come ready made signed by mother nature. Unalterable. Like preshrunk clothes, colorfast dyes. I'm shockproof as far as ugly women are concerned, they arrive at the airport after a flight of eleven or twelve hours, go to the bathroom and come out made up, lips red, hair curled, perfumed, so many vampires. Let me go into this room. Don't refuse me the services I'm ready to pay generously for.

—Juan, don't get desperate. A monster, that's something hard to come by. They don't occur often in nature and now we don't collect them in institutions. Who knows, perhaps the monster women live hidden some place we don't know about. If in actual fact you want that type of morsel, you won't find it here. Since we started the campaign of beautifying the city we put almost anyone in here. The truth is I'm happy to leave because I believe this outfit is, if you will pardon the expression, going to the devil. The other day I ran across a kid, a girl, and if I didn't hold the position I do, I'd hire her for my private office. Some have gaunt faces and graceful bodies, some are like a tub of lard, chubby, with a rank odor of perspiration cured after the first cold shower. Out of favoritism a bunch of harebrained boys no good for any other type of work has been contracted as agents. They have relatives in the ministry and when they hit the streets they pick up anybody who should be interned, according to their unscientific standards. And later come the bribes to get rid of undesirable elements like that dame, the owner of the Academy, who denounced all her employees to whom she owed compensation or the husbands tired of lying to their lovers, aunts saddled with insolent orphans who keep remembering their real parents. On the other hand there are rich ugly women who go about in total freedom. This is a mess, my friend, but at least it offers the advantage of a high concentration of female bodies right here, so you'll have ample possibilities for choosing. You have to hurry, it's nearly dawn, soon it'll be light.

—I insist on knowing what's behind that door; I believe that with the sum I'm paying you can confide in me, make an exception.

—Nothing easier to manage, my dear Juan. Two crazy women. That's all. One came denounced by her own husband, Josefina de la Puente. She talks to herself, sings, dances, gets the young ones stirred up. They say she's the one who started the habit of all peeing at the same time after the assemblies; doesn't the stench bother you? I'm used to it now but I notice your eyes are irritated, it must be because of that. Once you leave, it'll go away. Keep your eyes closed for two hours, put some compresses of tepid tea on them, you know how to do it? First cut a piece of gauze, put it aside, boil the water . . .

—And the other one? Who is she? Why are they together?

—The other is a very sad case. Marisa Format. Excellent lawyer. Woman active in all areas of the institutional life of the city. A privileged individual with some impressive curves. During the rainy season it was impossible for her to get her dose of elixir and she went into a state of almost total catatonia after a dreadful crisis of convulsions. But you, Juan, a porter, you wouldn't understand much of these things. Let's go on, you must make your selection.

—And why do you have them shut up here together?

—Look, you just don't know when to stop. Because we don't have time
  we're in a hurry
    we have urgent business
      our appointments
        our tennis games
a doctor is not a lady's companion
  a doctor is   diploma   pride   salary   double-breasted suit
a doctor should not attend to whimsical hysterical crises

let the privileged ladies take care of themselves
let them croak
—A lovely tune, and I thought you were self-sacrificing types.
—Now you see how skewed the world is when you get away from airports, you should spend more time in the street. But of course with that mole . . .

Rogelio had heard the entire conversation. Excited by the chance to see Josefina again, he crouched behind a pile of gray blankets, waiting for someone from the cleaning staff to open the door of the room, which was not even locked, despite its appearance.

every time I go on the merry-go-round I get dizzy

The Secretary in Charge of Maintaining Public Order announces to all members of the population that they must refrain from going into the street after ten o'clock in the evening and there will be
- no talking on the telephone
- no purchasing of foreign-made goods
- no selling of loafers
- no buying of loafers
- no consuming of loafers
- no organizing of meetings of any kind
- no harboring of minors under eighteen years of age who are not members of the family
- no traveling in four-wheeled vehicles
- no staying out of bed after eleven in the evening

Anyone not observing these orders will be shot immediately without a trial.

life's so much nicer in hotels

Clara recovered from her chills, shyness, and arthritis quickly enough to realize that Teresa was a chatterbox and not very bright. The first indication was when Teresa called her with loud shrieks from the next room because she'd dropped the bills into the toilet. They fished them out as well as they could, washed them, and pressed them with a warm iron that one of the waiters brought them, since the electricity had come back on. Clara had little interest in where all that money came from. What she wanted for sure was to leave right away. She must go to the port, she had an appointment, she knew it. With the sailor suit spread over a chair, Clara tried to talk Teresa into asking Armando for some sort of vehicle. They were so far away. She no longer wanted to hitchhike or take public transportation. A certain impatience caused her to play with the belt of the chinese-silk bathrobe that Armando had given each of them the night they arrived. Teresa, as you can imagine, didn't want to go anywhere. Between the guerrillas and Armando, her world had become densely populated. Gustavo, a short dark Guatemalan, followed her through the ballrooms of the hotel with proposals of an idyllic triangle with Armando as the financial backer and involving only the slightest sexual elements. Teresa was enchanted. She felt flattered, appreciated; the mysterious nature of Clara's search grew dim at times to give way to plans for a brilliant future as the Guatemalan's *compañera* in revolutionary ventures involving trips to rural villages where they would avoid the photographers and sit down to eat typical dishes in clandestine camps whose inhabitants would welcome them, eyes filled with tears, and greet her while commenting in whispers of admiration on her expensive clothes, because Armando, it goes without saying, would treat her like a queen, give her priceless jewels snatched from the hotel safe after their owners, poisoned by the arsenic the cooks would inevitably put in their cheese tarts with a strawberry on top, were turned over to their grieving family members in a great hurry to claim their possessions. Gustavo said nothing to her about the future. Aside from the *compañeras* among the guerrillas, women aroused his hunter's instinct until he succeeded in making them succumb to his penetrating gaze. He didn't like to talk. Too much time spent in the underground. Let the gays do the talking. Up to now his eyes and in the dark his hands had been enough. Teresa's permanent wave, her false eyelashes involved him in an eminently feasible plan. One night, the third of his pursuit, Teresa sighed and told him that if need be she'd follow him to the ends of the earth.

—To the ends of the earth, no. We stay here. In my room.
—What I mean is I'm, well, ready for anything.
—Then let's go.
—Don't I have to pack my bags? Armando might suspect something, better to take nothing. Anyway, the rural population is going to give us what we need at first and with the money and the jewels . . . but for that we'll have to wait awhile. Oh, I'm so confused.
—That's it, you're confused, darling. To my room. It's only a couple of steps.

Teresa and Gustavo are heading for one of those rooms with an open balcony handy for transporting arms shipments. She looks into his eyes while he undresses. He takes off his clothes himself because it's such a complicated process; the boots, the pants with special pockets and buttons, the hunting rifle, the pistol, the Swiss-army knife to clean his nails and to cut fruit and cheese—from my point of view that knife is a sign of Gustavo's considerable practical side that distinguishes him from so many other mere revolutionaries with their heads in the clouds. When their clothes are all in a heap Teresa is an exquisite figure but Gustavo has shrunk down to eyes only. Maybe that's why it doesn't matter to Teresa when Armando comes from behind the curtain and says to Gustavo, *Many thanks, you can go, take your clothes and put something on, I don't want you to blame me for catching a cold like you did the last time.*

interview interruptus

—We'd like you to tell us who you are and why you and your group are after Teresa and why you haven't gone through official channels to find her.

—(Rafa in a falsetto voice) Who I am is of no importance. I'm one of the many women betrayed by that thieving female. We wish to find her and impeach her. We're not interested in having her put in jail. We want to have her for ourselves to subject her to the full force of our discipline.

—But if it's only a question of a mere theft . . .

—The discipline of the cell requires a special morality, a collective spirit. In betraying our trust, she's committed one of the worst crimes, causing the young members to question their faith in our organization.

—We understand that you personally are not acquainted with Teresa. You're a newcomer who's been given the leadership without anyone ever seeing your face. This aspect of the cell has surprised many members of the public at large; do you have any comment, any explanation to offer in this respect?

—To understand the reason for my anonymity one must analyze the situation prevailing in our city from the point of view of the Institute. The shawl across my face is a way to protect myself from the scrutiny of the agents of the Institute

I recommend that all women cover themselves
hide themselves
spend money on one single shawl
perhaps another as a spare
and forget about expensive cosmetics

—Don't get overexcited, we have no doctor on call here at the station. We've noted down everything and will repeat it with emphasis if you request it. Let's talk about the cell's future plans.

—Ah, that is very problematical because the cell is that, a cell, and not the whole body. We are part of the vast network of the international women's movement, a minuscule part of a great social transformation that will usher in the new century.

Rafa rolled his eyes, threw his head back, and was immediately recognized by Roberto, who in great indignation snatched off the disguise in front of everybody, leaving Rafa in his undershorts before the microphones. The radio listeners didn't realize anything had happened because a quick-witted announcer began to give the weather forecast, a lengthy process since the rainy season, which took at least half an hour of explanations and statistics. The journalists surrounded Rafa to save him from the fury of his followers, who were threatening him with the sickness by spitting in his face and eyes. Damp, covered with acrimonious saliva and scratches, Rafa went back to his house because he had an appointment. The minions of the cell decided he was certainly the one who'd stolen the money and set about to search for Teresa to beg her pardon, console her, and help her avenge herself against Rafa.

whose eye is it and whose tooth?

LATE-BREAKING NEWS

The savage killer of the boy has been apprehended red-handed while attempting to strangle an innocent, ten-year-old minor.

A certain Walter Fernández residing in the capital has been apprehended by the authorities and accused of killing the boy who died in unexplained circumstances four months ago. At the time of his arrest the accused was attempting to strangle the minor Flora Indurain, whose screams and protests attracted the attention of the numerous youths who congregate in the area called Barrio del Ángel on the outskirts of the city. Fernández was attempting to steal a paper the girl had hidden in her school bag. The authorities have established that in the aforementioned document Fernández admits his guilt of the earlier crime. In a press conference the Chief of Police thanked all sectors of the population for the cooperation they received in this matter.

Flora Indurain receives a medal from the League of Women

In a meeting to take place in the Teatro del Campo the twentieth of this month at six o'clock the Medal of Valor and Bravery will be given to the minor Flora Indurain. In attendance at the ceremony will be religious and civic leaders as well as representatives of various international women's organizations.

Marked improvement in the health of Dr. Format

A spokesman for the Institute of Rehabilitation has announced that Dr. Format will resume her work in the course of the next month. The diagnosis of her illness points to a severe allergic reaction to the food served in the Institute of Beautification of the City. A probe into the sanitary conditions of the establishment in question is under way. Dr. Format will assume the leadership of the investigating commission as soon as she has fully recovered, according to a statement by her secretary.

What can I tell you? It left me speechless

Rogelio spent hours and days in front of the door behind which Marisita and Josefina could be found. Various times he tried to enter just after their breakfast was brought or their room was being cleaned, but something kept him from stepping over the threshold. He thought of all the times he'd eaten Josefina's meatballs. The memory made his mouth water. He remembered the summer sessions in the hammock and had various erections but it was no use. Nothing had prepared him to save Josefina. He was afraid she wouldn't recognize him. He felt he was drowning every time the door opened and he sensed her perfume. He was there when Marisita came out on her way to the dining room holding Josefina's arm.

—Walk, Filomena, it'll do you good. Walk, a little more and you'll be dancing and singing.

—Many thanks, Señora de la Puente. I repeat that my name is Marisa Format. I'm your lawyer. Don't you remember? I'm going to get you out of here, I want you to be my secretary.

—Yes, yes, yes, Filomena, I'm going with you. I promised you, I'll take you to a restaurant, teach you about our typical dishes, and later we race off to the Amazon. I always wanted to live with the Indians. What an opportunity! I've seen so many movies, and yet never thought I'd succeed in having my dream come true. The problem is knowing when to go and how to get there. We'll figure it out, as my late husband used to say. We'll figure it out.

—But your husband's not dead, Señora de la Puente. He had you institutionalized, that's all. Here, to keep you from being put in the insane asylum. You'll have to talk with Rogelio, Josefina. To clarify the situation.

—Clarify the situation! What fancy lawyers' talk! Don't be a lawyer with me, Filomena, it doesn't suit you, we already have enough impostors in the Institute. We don't need any more.

Rogelio had heard everything. Devastated behind the blankets, he wanted to start a revealing dance that would bring him close to Josefina but they moved away, chatting cheerfully. Josefina with a light step, rejuvenated, insisting on the trip to the Amazon, the plants, birds, waterfalls, rivers, little lakes, monkeys she thought she'd see, paint, enjoy; Marisita with eyes clear, cured of the elixir, ready for the Institute of Rehabilitation. *Later, when she's working in the office,* Rogelio said to himself, *it will be easier. I'll bring her flowers, dress like an Indian, woo her.*

oh, the light you gave to my life

The littleoldlady waits patiently for Juan to return to his house. She's prepared apple turnovers and is now sitting in the kitchen, reading a fashion magazine. She's wearing a tailored suit of a flecked tweed, nylon stockings, and low-heeled, patent-leather shoes. She's put on red lipstick and cleaned her tortoise-shell glasses. She's lovely, the nurses of the hospital have noticed it and also the surgeon, who's already declared his matrimonial intentions. Her financial situation has improved remarkably since she's paid off her hospital bill and can save her entire salary. She senses the key in the lock and, without being startled, waits until Juan sees her.

—It can't be . . . you

—Yes, I've come to visit you, to clear things up

—Look, if you're thinking about turning me in, let me tell you right away that I have all the money with me. I was thinking of using it to make a purchase, buy something to fulfill an old dream of mine . . . But I repented. I don't want, you know, **I don't want** someone to pull the wool over my eyes again, leave me stranded. And then better not even to try, because not one of them was ugly enough and would've walked out no matter how grateful they might've been for the luxuries I could give them.

—Luxuries? You?

—And how. With your money. I was going to buy them and with what was left over have them live like queens but it won't work. It won't work. Look, don't turn me in. Or do whatever you please. I have everything here, **intact**, except for what I had to pay for the ticket for that deserter Dr. Danilo; that one, now, he's really a case. And imagine I believed so much studying would make a person different, educated, honest. I'll give you all the money I have and the rest I'll pay in installments because the tourist season is just beginning and I'll have to see how well they tip. More than to anyone else. They say my mole makes a big impression and they want me to get out of their sight quick . . . that way there's no problem, in a few months you'll recoup bill by bill . . .

Juan took out the patent leather purse that matched the shoes exactly. The littleoldlady, excited, jumped from her chair and exclaimed:

—So you were also searching for me, darling, you also, like me, and you saved me from the pickpocket who snatched my purse when I had the heart attack. What sensitivity! Now we can go wherever you wish, get to know one another, play poker, go to amusement parks. A turnover, try a turnover, my love, your face is very pale. You look like you're about to faint. Here, sit beside me in this chair. I'll make you some tea. Let's not talk about anything. You have to recover from the shock. The surgeon told me. The best way to avoid another heart attack is to be careful of shocks.

I'll give it to you straight

—Latin Lover, from now on that's what you'll call me.
—Forever?
—Oh, you women! Why do you want to know till when? Armando, your Latin Lover.
—But I thought that Lover meant we'd consummated our affair, and you, well, after all . . .
—For the purpose of the radio program I will be the Lover. We have to let the public imagine things and we do what we wish, because I do wish, my love, how not wish with such a gorgeous girl? I stripped naked to take the wind out of the sails of that Guatemalan who puts my teeth on edge. Always showing off with his weapons. They're dirt-poor and have nothing until they get the stuffed envelopes from the governments in exile; then they pay me and I give them paella, everything. But in between it's beer and french fries. To hell with them. A bunch of assholes who even chant those old-fashioned revolutionary songs off-key. . . .
—You think the *Engagements of Yesteryear* program is still going? And even if it were, it's illegal for the participants to know one another. If I remember right, the littleoldlady had never seen the one who played her sweetheart. . . .
—We'll do something different. We have talent
   a plan
     a future
   fame to forge
   photographs
     press conferences
Sing, sing with me . . .
—I'm cold. I want to get dressed.
—No, not that. Absolutely not. We have to look at each other, get to know each other intimately. You, I gather, are somewhat untruthful, my duckling. I've learned that when people are wearing no clothes they always tell the truth.

—At least let me get under the covers. I'm getting the shivers. Look at the goose bumps.

—Just like the drenched duckling, the way my mother told me.

The conversation between Teresa and Armando lasted for hours. At first she didn't know how to respond to his questions because up to then her answers had concerned the sort of clothes she wore, the effect she wanted to make with her words. She rarely stopped to examine facts. Time flew as she made sure her hair was smooth, her lipstick well applied. Armando examined her with hermit eyes. He exuded an isolation of centuries, and Teresa gradually felt a growing respect for the mission he'd invented for the two of them.

—Fine. I'll go back to the city. I'll call the program and when I hear the voice of the Latin Lover I'll pretend to be surprised. We'll stay tuned in for months.

—And years. I can't wait; the flood of letters and telegrams with the stories of the city already burn in my hands. Mornings I'll answer them with a special pencil, a quill pen. I'll be photographed nude, pen in hand, and nobody will realize I'm not a mythological character.

Fruitcake, madder than a hatter, Teresa would have said to him some years earlier but now she was ready to accept anything, and since Clara had already forgotten her existence, she took the train ticket Armando handed her and headed back to the city.

farewells

Rita is a goddess before the crowd. Behind her the banker keeps picking up each one of the garments she removes in her slow striptease. She'll stop only when, in the middle of the demonstration, the bemedaled and still sleepless Flora appears carrying Amandita, whom she'd found in a garbage can after Camila absentmindedly let her go crawling off alone.

    Enough garbage
        enough exhibitionism
            enough plump women in search of fortune
        enough edicts and filth

She's flanked by clerics of various religions. All of them want to be with the young, get some advantage out of it, let people know they're still up-to-date but the crowd, eager to see Rita's body, is primed for the bra and the panties when the banker, quick, efficient, starts throwing slips of colored paper into the air giving the place where Rita's movies are shown. With a fur coat thrown quickly around her shoulders, Rita exits, blowing kisses. But the kids of the Barrio del Ángel march on the radio station. They want to take it over, read a communiqué to the people. Too much of a mess, it can't be done so quickly. You don't take power that way, my dears. You have to wait. A gradual democratic process, the clerics say. The last time I went by there, the kids were standing guard in the hallways.

secrets

The beauty queens without make-up brought in by the Institute's agents have joined the plotters and now, instead of wanting to get out, they're all working on an immense publicity campaign to attract volunteer internees. The neglect and corruption of the staff, the fear of probes and investigations thought up by Dr. Format and her assistant, Josefina, have contributed to the exodus of the leadership team. The self-governing system has been of benefit to the enterprising girls who broadcast on radio news of the excellent treatment and cures available to restore both physical and mental health, all without any male presence. Women come from all parts of that city, which is now orderly at last. However, to find the rhythm of one's own lungs, the ticktock of the soul requires breathing very deeply. Few can do it. Camila walks the streets looking for Rogelio so he can help her, but we know, we sense, he's whirling in circles in his eternal search for the doorknob. Elena has foreseen that Amandita will become president and is sewing gala clothes for her, which she sends to the Barrio del Ángel through certain intermediaries, privileged girls with reddish-green eyes. Only Clara, now back from the port, waits on a bench as she had imagined from the beginning. Roberto will come to the square but will not see her because Peggy has made him close his eyes so as to concentrate better on perfecting his pronunciation of Nahuatl.

Marisita and Josefina de la Puente have left by plane for the Amazon jungle. Years, perhaps centuries, will pass before they're found, luscious, mocking, dancing with an Arab on the lookout for oil and Indian girls with jet-black hair. They're happy, they wave to us before the curtain goes down, and if we're not too busy at that hour, we could go with them to search for what they found.

Interview with Alicia Borinsky

JULIO ORTEGA: *Dreams of the Abandoned Seducer*, first of all, makes the reader into an accomplice by means of its ironic freedom. The humor turns daily life into a spectacle. Are the men and women in your novel true to life in the Buenos Aires scene or are they figures of satirical pleasantry?

ALICIA BORINSKY: Some readers say they have found in *Dreams* a neighbor, an enemy, a collection of phrases and tics that they recognize from the urban scene. And I say "urban scene" or "landscape" because the daily life I imagine in this novel takes place in an invented city similar to other cities with *porteño* roots but not limited to Buenos Aires. One example would be the obsession and fascination regarding physical beauty that leads to the internment of the ugly women in *Dreams*. The persistence of the evaluating look that measures hips, admires hairdos, notices the acne, establishes hierarchies is omnipresent in Latin America and throughout the Mediterranean countries. That's why the reality of going out into the street and taking that experience as a more or less conscious visit to the theater is part of the way people live in many places, not only in Buenos Aires. Certainly Buenos Aires may be more intense in that regard with the ubiquity of the male look and address to women in the street through a *piropo*, a gallant remark, or an aggressive erotic comment. In this novel I exaggerate something that is an integral part of that curiosity and rivalry played out in the streets almost as though they were a battleground, a training camp for the practice of gossip, a pretext for an exercise in style. I do not believe that the strongly humorous aspect of my work goes against the verisimilitude of its characters. On the contrary, it seems to me that what the *porteños* call "cargada," an unpleasant practical joke at the expense of someone else, can reveal to us our own nature.

JO: Macedonio's lighthearted absurdities and Puig's skepticism

Alicia Borinsky, interview by Julio Ortega, Boston, Massachusetts, January 1997. In Spanish, published in *Brújula/Compass* 27 (Spring 1997).

concerning individuality and his preference for certain types and stereotypes seem to appear in your novel. Are you in a dialogue with them and with other masters of the art of the antiheroic narration?

AB: Macedonio and Puig are constants in much of what I write; they have left me in a quandary with respect to the role of the voice in fiction. Macedonio has a witty eloquence, revealed in those conversations with the readers where he dares them, tries to instruct them, imagines them skipping pages, while Puig invents a totally different atmosphere; his key is to be found in common sense and in sentimentalism. Both aspects appear in my work in a dialogue that was real in the case of Puig, since we were friends, and from a familiarity with the work and milieu in the case of Macedonio. I like Puig's stereotypes, that doubleplay of the psychological with the paradoxes of a prudent middle-class life where pettiness turns into an avalanche of set phrases, women who spy on their neighbors, girls who fall in love with cheap Don Juans. The practice of the absurd in Macedonio allows one to find cracks in Puig's passion for the everyday and the claustrophobia of its language. Puig and Macedonio are masters of dialogue, each with a very distinct style. The particular idiom of *Dreams* is forged in that theater of whispers and fictional encounters where I work, together with Lewis Carroll, Felisberto Hernández, Nina Berberova, Clarice Lispector, certain children's stories, tangos that tell us about the intricacies of love and women's lives, Mexican boleros of the *época dorada* (golden age); to a certain degree my volume of poetry *Madres alquiladas* (Rent-a-Mom) speaks that language as well. These are at least the ones I'm consciously aware of; some readers have found echoes of others more familiar to them and when they tell me what they are, those, in turn, become mine.

JO: What urban social landscape is represented in this novel?

Is it the Buenos Aires of imagined roles that Puig invented? Perhaps the Buenos Aires of Menem, middle-class, and free-market?

AB: It always makes me a bit uncomfortable, the identification of contemporary Latin American literature with magical realism and its concomitant privilege of a rural aspect bent on the picturesque and the folkloric, which is, of course, there and has given us works of the highest quality and broadened our imagination, but is not, I believe, the only kind of writing that characterizes our literatures at the moment. I am fascinated by the shapes that lives acquire in present-day cities, the possibilities for confusion and love in a space where the fragmentation of family life and the new social incarnations of women suggest prospects for crisscrossed stories, conflicts that are resolved in nonlinear, sometimes absurd, ways. Dreams takes place in an invented city with characteristics of many. The commercial and administrative fever of the novel's characters that impels some of them, for example, to establish an alternative prostitution service for men who, tired of the erotic excesses of their independent and very modern wives, frequent an institution where there are women who mend their socks and prepare their favorite foods—a situation that is exaggerated in the novel but that builds on something present in our societies. The new economic realities of the market feed the frantic rhythm of Dreams with its celebration and dark parody of chances for selling and buying practically anything; the Buenos Aires of today exudes this atmosphere, as do other cities in different parts of the world that are just now plunging wildly into the free-market economy. In this sense I do not believe that my Buenos Aires resembles Puig's very much. There is one aspect of the urban imagination that brings us close to one another. It rests on the intimacy of the bond between characters and on the contact with the reader through the direct use of a nonintellectualized way of talking. Neither in Puig's city nor in mine is there too much fondness for high-flown rhetoric. That's why I make such frequent use of tangos and boleros (some made up by me).

JO: At times we readers of your novel feel the author is close at hand, laughing along with us. That complicity—what is being suggested here?

AB: To play. Dance. Make friends with the reader, to think we all belong to the same circle and that our relationship makes it possible for us to take in the ridiculous side of life instead of avoiding it. I've always mistrusted the type of arrogant humor that punishes in order to privilege the voice that is speaking, the joke that leaves the joker untouched. Most of the jokes that we accept and enjoy come from that attitude, and women are often the chosen target for arrogant humor. My writing, I hope, gives a suggestive and sexualized clue to what is said without the aspect of exclusion; reader and author are integrated into the flow of dialogue as part of that situation. In addition, I work permanently under the illusion that there's something illuminating in gradually undoing the invisible strings that attach us to the commonplaces said by people around us. It's not only that I include the readers deliberately, but also the expression of my need to believe that in the fictions I construct I am part of a friendly, rollicking alliance. That's why the writing of *Dreams* involved setting up a special place in my study, with music, photographs, faces of movie actors and actresses, and even clothes that I wore for the novel. That effort does not imply anything artificial on my part; it's like furnishing a house or creating a set for a play. When I go into my study, I enter the world I share with the readers, and knowing I have their company, the act of dismantling the lies that form the substrate of everyday language turns into an exercise we perform together. If that were not so, all this dark humor would indeed be shattering. There is—and let's not forget it—a fierce and hungry counterpart to the kind of revelation elicited by guffaws that could very well leave us speechless. *Dreams* invites its readers to participate because they're already there in a sense and have been from the beginning, articulating the tone of the novel. Among the photos in my study is one of Buster Keaton. His deadpan expression and imperturbability and my perplexity before that mystery accessible to the young in the form of the constant temptation to laugh, to say, "I am putting you on," were part of the impulse of the writing. I do not think the novel shows nostalgia for any particular era or age; it is, on the contrary, cast toward today and tomorrow. Because I like the profound involvement in play we all experience when we are young and that most of us lose as time goes by, I wanted to bring back some of that energy for adults. That's the reason for the nonpunitive sexuality of *Dreams* and for its ending dictated by a logic that has to be ferreted out, as in a detective story.

Translated by Cola Franzen and Alicia Borinsky

In the Latin American Women Writers series

Underground River and Other Stories
By Inés Arredondo
Translated by Cynthia Steele
With a foreword by Elena Poniatowska

Dreams of the Abandoned Seducer: Vaudeville Novel
By Alicia Borinsky
Translated by Cola Franzen in
collaboration with the author
with a foreword by Cola Franzen and an
interview with Julio Ortega

Mean Woman
By Alicia Borinsky
Translated and with an
introduction by Cola Franzen

The Fourth World
By Diamela Eltit
Translated and with a
foreword by Dick Gerdes

The Women of Tijucopapo
By Marilene Felinto
Translated and with an
afterword by Irene Matthews

The Youngest Doll
By Rosario Ferré

Industrial Park: A Proletarian Novel
By Patrícia Galvão (Pagu)
Translated by Elizabeth Jackson and
K. David Jackson

DISCARDED